The Library Ghost

The Library Ghost

GORDON SNELL

POOLBEG

Published 2000 by
Poolbeg Press Ltd,
123 Baldoyle Industrial Estate,
Dublin 13, Ireland
E-mail: poolbeg@poolbeg.com
www.poolbeg.com

A catalogue record for this book is available from the British Library.

ISBN 1 85371 909 9

Cover design by Artmark
Set by Pat Hope
Printed and bound in Great Britain by
Cox & Wyman Ltd., Reading, Berkshire.

About the Author

Gordon Snell is a well-known scriptwriter and author of books for children and adults. Other books in the series include *Dangerous Treasure, The Mystery of Monk Island, The Curse of Werewolf Castle, The Phantom Horseman, The Case of the Mystery Graves* and *The Secret of the Circus.* He is also the author of *The Tex & Sheelagh Omnibus.* He lives in Dalkey, Co. Dublin, and is married to the writer Maeve Binchy.

DEDICATION:
For dearest Maeve, with all my love

1

A Mysterious Book

"Of course, in years to come, they'll be as extinct as dinosaurs," said Brendan, as he and his cousin Molly and their friend Dessy walked along the main street in Ballygandon.

"What will?" asked Molly.

"Those," said Brendan, pointing to the books Molly was carrying. They were on their way to the library so that Molly could change her books.

"I sometimes wish books *were* extinct," said Dessy. "School would be a lot more fun. We could spend the whole time in class telling jokes to each other."

"If they were *your* jokes, Dessy," Molly said, "everyone would be mitching from school the whole time."

"Seriously," said Brendan, "books will soon be a thing of the past. Everyone will have little hand-held computers, and just slot a disc into them with a whole book on it, then read it off the screen."

"I'd still prefer a book," said Molly.

The library was one of the oldest buildings in Ballygandon. It had once been a gate-lodge at an entrance to the grounds of the ruined castle which stood on the hill outside the town – the castle where the three of them, the 'Ballygandon Gang' had had many adventures. The castle was supposed to be haunted by the spirit of Princess Ethna, who had been murdered there on the night before her wedding, several centuries ago.

The library was a stone building, and the door opened straight into a large, tall room with shelves all around it and rows of shelves in the centre too. There were smaller rooms off it. One was the office of Joan Bright, the librarian, another had a computer where people could log on to the Internet to find out information. Visitors to the town sometimes used it to pick up their e-mails too.

Joan Bright was at the counter just near the entrance, where books were checked in and out. She was a small, round woman who wore large, pink glasses and had her ginger-coloured hair always in a neat, wavy style. She had worked in the library here for more than thirty years, but she had never lost her love of books. She was eager that children should love them too, so she let them wander around among the shelves as much as they liked, browsing or sitting reading on the chairs and large cushions that were scattered around.

She held regular story-telling sessions, when she or

sometimes a visiting author would read to groups of children. The audiences enjoyed Miss Bright's readings as much as anyone's: she acted out the stories as she read, gesturing and taking on different voices for each of the characters.

"Hello there," she said, as they came into the library. "So you're here again to see us, Brendan and Dessy."

"It's the holidays," said Molly. "Besides, they much prefer Ballygandon to dirty old Dublin, don't you, fellas?"

"There's nothing wrong with Dublin, it's a grand city," said Dessy, reluctant to admit that he had a lot more fun on his frequent visits to Ballygandon than he did at home.

Molly handed in her two books. "Have you got any more by her?" she asked, pointing at one of them.

"Yes, there's a new one just out," said Miss Bright. "You'll be the first reader."

"Great," said Molly, "I'll go and find it. Meanwhile, Brendan can tell you his idea of how there won't be any books left at all in a few years' time."

Molly grinned, as Brendan said stumblingly: "Well, I didn't mean that, exactly. I mean there would still have to be libraries . . ."

"Well, that's a relief," said Miss Bright, "or I'd be out of a job. So what kind of library will I be running, Brendan?"

Dessy drifted away to look at the shelves, leaving Brendan to deal with the question on his own. Miss Bright listened to Brendan politely, and answered seriously that she thought he might be right that books would be on computer discs – in fact many already were. But she said people had predicted that books would be out of date, many times before. They said radio, and later television, would mean that no one would read any more. But books still survived.

"You see, Brendan," she said, "I think books are what you computer experts call 'user-friendly' – attractive objects in themselves and very easy to use. You don't need any electronics or programs or buttons and keys, you just open the page and away you go."

Brendan was flattered to be called a computer expert, and he certainly wasn't going to try to argue any further.

Molly had gone to find her book, while Dessy had made straight for the Humour section to see if he could pick up any more jokes. They heard him give a cry of shock.

"What's up, Dessy?" said Molly, peering round the corner of the bookstack.

Dessy was pointing at the shelves. He was laughing now. "Just for a moment, I thought I'd seen a ghost. Look!"

Molly moved towards him, and Brendan joined them. There was a gap in the books on one of the shelves. From it, two yellow eyes were gazing out at them.

"That's Internet!" laughed Molly. "She's the library

cat. Hello, Internet!" She reached in and stroked the cat, which gave a *miaow* of pleasure, then jumped off the shelf and down onto a high stool nearby. She was a big fluffy cat, all black except for her white paws. She looked as if she was wearing socks.

"Aren't you a beautiful cat?" said Molly, stroking her head. Internet put her head back and gave a gigantic yawn. "That's a greeting, in Cat-Speak," said Molly.

"You could have fooled me," said Dessy.

"So you found Internet," said Miss Bright, coming up to them. "She's handsome, isn't she? She came here two years ago – just wandered in and decided to stay."

"Internet – that's a great name," said Dessy.

"I called her that because she used to sleep on top of the computer. But now she seems to prefer finding a snug place on the shelves."

"Dessy thought he'd seen a ghost," said Molly.

"Only for a second," said Dessy. "Those yellow eyes were all I could see."

"There are no ghosts here," said Miss Bright. "At least . . ." She paused uncertainly.

"Have you seen anything?" Brendan was excited.

"No," said Miss Bright. "it's just that a few times I've arrived here in the morning, and found some of the books disturbed – fallen off the shelves, and so on. Almost as though someone was looking for something, and pushed them off in annoyance."

"Maybe it was Internet, looking for some good jokes," said Dessy.

"I thought it might be the cat, but it doesn't happen in this section." She moved to a far corner of the library, and they followed. Internet came along too. "It's always over here, in the Local History section. There are lots of books here about Ballygandon, and especially about the castle and its history."

"Like the story of Princess Ethna?" said Molly.

"Exactly. In fact there was an old document found buried under a cupboard in the basement when we were doing some cleaning-up down there. It was written in Old Irish and it was hard to read, but it looked like a diary of some kind."

"Maybe it was Ethna's diary?" said Molly eagerly.

"I don't know. We are not even sure it was really old at all. I sent it to the experts in Dublin to be examined. I'm expecting their report soon."

"And suppose it *is* the real thing, what will happen to it?" asked Brendan.

"Well, what I'd like to do is to stage a special exhibition in the library, and after that it might go on tour to other libraries and museums. It could help to bring in some funds for books. All the public libraries are starved for funds these days."

"If it's real, the diary must be very valuable," said Molly.

"Oh, it would be worth a fortune," said Joan Bright, "but of course it could never be sold. It would be a national treasure."

"Can we help you with the exhibition?" asked

Brendan. "I could take some special pictures of the castle."

"And I could maybe make a model and paint it," said Molly.

Dessy didn't know what to suggest he could do. He thought of saying he'd be happy to show off some of his yo-yo tricks, but it didn't sound as if that would be quite the right thing.

"We'll find something for you to do too, Dessy," said Miss Bright kindly. "Thank you all. The problem is, it may be a while before I can organize the exhibition. My mother is very sick, and she's going to need full-time looking after for a while. So I have asked for a month's leave of absence."

"Will the library have to close?" asked Brendan.

"No, they've found a librarian who's volunteered to replace me. She's called Evanna Carr. I don't know her, but I am sure she will manage fine. I'll show her where everything is."

"Including Internet?" Molly smiled as she leaned down to stroke the cat.

"Including Internet. She's part of the fixtures by now. And she's no trouble."

Internet gave a *miaow*, as if she agreed with this praise.

When they got back to Molly's house, they went into the shop her parents ran, hoping to cadge a few sweets from Molly's mother. But Mrs O'Rourke was at the counter, buying some cigarettes. They didn't care for Mrs O'Rourke, who had a number of horse-drawn caravans she hired out to tourists. She had been involved in some shady dealings around the area, including trying to sell a field for houses – a field which didn't belong to her at all.

"Did you get some new books at the library?" Molly's mother asked.

"I did," said Molly, showing the two she was carrying. "See you later, Mam."

The three of them went through the door at the back of the shop, which led into the house.

Just as she was closing the door, Molly heard Mrs O'Rourke say: "I'm surprised that library keeps going at all, with a librarian like that."

Molly kept the door ajar and listened. Her mother said: "Joan Bright? I think she's very nice. The children certainly like her."

"Well, they would, wouldn't they? She lets them run around the place just as they like. It's amazing half the books aren't pinched or torn to bits."

"I hope you're not talking about Molly and her friends?" said Molly's mother sharply.

"I'm not singling anyone out," said Mrs O'Rourke. "But I do think that Miss Bright is past it. She's been there too long. She's too hung up on all those local legends and history and stuff. She probably believes there are ghosts walking round the place. She's getting a bit odd, if you ask me."

"I wasn't asking you, Mrs O'Rourke," said Molly's mother coldly.

"Suit yourself," said Mrs O'Rourke, and she turned and went out of the shop.

"That woman is a pest," Molly told Brendan and Dessy. "If she's slagging off poor Miss Bright, we're going to have to watch her."

"We'll watch her all right," said Brendan. "After all, we're the Ballygandon Private Eyes!"

2

Basement Secrets

"Could you just take this lot of books over to the Fiction section and put them in their places?" asked Joan Bright, pointing to a pile of books on the counter. "Then I do believe we're finished."

It was the day Miss Bright was starting her leave of absence. Molly, Brendan and Dessy were helping her do a final tidying up in the library, ready for the arrival of Evanna Carr to take over from her.

"Thank you for all your help," said Miss Bright, when they had put the books on the shelves. "Well, the place is really spick and span now. We just have to wait for Miss Carr."

"While we're waiting," said Molly, "I was wondering . . ."

"Yes, Molly?" said Miss Bright.

"Could we have a look in the basement, where you found Princess Ethna's diary?"

10

"I don't see why not," said Miss Bright, "though remember, we don't know yet whether that's what the document is."

She led them across the big room to a door in the far corner near the Local History section. She opened it, and they could see some rickety-looking wooden stairs leading down into the darkness.

"It looks spooky." said Dessy. "Maybe that's where the ghost lives." Then he called in a hollow voice: *"Hello there!"*

"Stop acting the eejit, Dessy," said Molly.

"Look!" said Miss Bright, reaching for a switch beside the door. The basement lit up. "Not a ghost in sight! Now be careful going down the stairs. I'd better wait in the library for Miss Carr to arrive."

They went slowly down the stairs, and found themselves in a dusty, low-ceilinged room with stone walls and a stone floor. There were a few shelves on the walls with boxes on them, and some alcoves in the walls, one with a tall cupboard in it.

"Even with the light on it still feels spooky enough," said Brendan.

"Hey," said Dessy, "here's a good riddle for you. What song do they sing in the graveyard playground?"

"You're going to tell us, aren't you, Dessy?" said Molly wearily.

"Boys and Ghouls Come Out To Play!" said Dessy.

"You'd have the ghosts in fits," said Molly.

"I wonder what's in here," said Brendan. He opened the door of the big cupboard. It creaked loudly. There were only two empty shelves in the cupboard, covered in dust. There was no back to it, just the stone wall of the basement. There was a shallow hole in the floor of the cupboard where some of the stones had been moved away. Brendan knelt down and looked into it.

"This must be where they found the diary," said Brendan. "It looks as if it has been dug out quite recently."

"Perhaps there are more things down there," said Molly. She put her hand into the hole and felt around. "It seems pretty solid, but if we could come back with a trowel or something, we might be able to dig a bit further."

"Princess Ethna might not like that," said Dessy.

They were all kneeling down now in front of the cupboard. Just as Dessy spoke, they heard a weird, wailing sound. They gasped, and looked around wildly.

"What was that?" said Brendan in alarm.

They stared round the basement. It seemed to be quite empty. Warily, they moved out into the middle of the room. Then they heard the wailing sound again.

"It came from over there," said Molly, pointing towards the stairs. She moved slowly to the stairs and peered underneath them. Then she laughed. "It's Internet!" she said. She reached in and took hold of the cat. She held it in her arms, stroking its head. The cat yawned.

"Have you come ghost-hunting with us?" asked Dessy. The cat miaowed.

"You see?" Dessy said. "She's talking to me."

"You'll be telling her jokes next," said Brendan.

"I'll give it a go," said Dessy. "Hey, Internet, what's the difference between . . . ?"

He was interrupted by a call from the top of the stairs. It was Miss Bright. *"Time to come up now!"* she said. "Miss Carr has arrived."

They went up the stairs, with Molly leading the way, carrying Internet. When she reached the top, the cat jumped out of her arms, and scuttled back down into the basement.

"Poor old Internet," said Miss Bright. "She's sometimes nervous of strangers."

"The basement is the best place for her," said a sharp voice behind her. "You wouldn't want a creature like that hanging round in a library."

When they came into the library, they saw Miss Carr for the first time. She was tall and thin, totally unlike Joan Bright. She had a sharp nose and black hair drawn back into a bun. She wore a well-cut grey jacket and skirt. She gazed at the emerging trio disapprovingly through steel-rimmed spectacles.

Miss Bright said: "I'd like you to meet some of our keenest young readers. Miss Carr, this is Molly, who lives in Ballygandon, and her cousin Brendan and their friend Dessy, from Dublin."

"How do you do?" said Molly, holding out her hand.

Miss Carr didn't take it. She simply nodded and said: "Nice to meet you." But she didn't sound as if she meant it. She turned to Miss Bright and said: "Well, let's get on with it, shall we? The sooner you show me where everything is, the sooner you can get away to see to your mother."

"Right," said Miss Bright.

Molly realised that if they stayed they would only annoy the new librarian. "Well, we'll be off then," she said.

"Thanks so much for all your help," Joan Bright told them. She said to Miss Carr: "These children are always happy to give a helping hand in the library. You can call on them any time."

"How nice," said Miss Carr coolly.

"Goodbye for now, then," said Molly to Miss Bright. "We'll come and see you."

"That would be lovely."

Brendan and Dessy said goodbye too, then Molly said: "Welcome to Ballygandon, Miss Carr. I'm sure we'll see you here in the library lots of times."

Miss Carr smiled a thin smile. The Ballygandon Gang left the library.

"Well, she was a real misery-boots, wasn't she?" said Dessy as they walked towards Molly's house. "Maybe I should tell her a few jokes to cheer her up."

"I'd have more chance of cheering her up with my tin whistle," said Molly, taking her whistle out and playing a tune as they walked.

"There won't be much chance of doing more

searching in the basement, with her around," said Brendan gloomily.

"Maybe we could sneak down there when she isn't looking," said Dessy.

"I think we should do that anyway, to make sure Internet is OK," said Molly. "It looks as if she'll have to live in the basement now, and I'm sure that Carr woman won't bother to feed her properly the way Miss Bright did."

"Hey," said Dessy, "how about this one? What do they call it when Miss Carr has a bath?"

"I give up, Dessy," said Brendan.

"A Car-Wash!" said Dessy. This time Molly and Brendan actually laughed. Dessy was pleased.

"Car-Wash, that's what we'll call her from now on," said Brendan.

They came to the yard outside Molly's parents' shop. A rattly old car came up the road and trundled into the yard. Brendan and Molly's grandfather stepped out and greeted them.

"Hi, Locky!" they all chorused.

"Hello there, Ballygandon Gang!" said Locky. "Is your mother around, Molly?"

"She's in the shop," said Molly.

She led the way and they all went into the shop. Molly's mother was delighted to see Locky.

Locky said: "Maureen, I wanted to have a bit of a chat with you about something."

He paused. Molly and the others looked on with interest, wondering what it was. But Locky didn't go on. Instead, he glanced in their direction, and Molly's mother took the hint.

"Go along, the three of you," said Molly's mother, "your grandfather and I want to have a word in private."

They went into the house, but her curiosity was too much for Molly. She kept the door ajar as she had yesterday, to listen to what Locky said. Brendan listened too.

What they heard was not good news. Locky said he was worried about Brendan's father. The newspaper he worked for was reducing its staff, and as Brendan's father was on a short contract, he might soon have to go. If that happened there would be a problem about keeping up the payments on the house. They might even have to sell it.

Brendan was very upset. He almost wished he hadn't overheard what Locky said. But it was no good ignoring things. They must think of some way of saving his father's job.

"But what can we do?" said Dessy. "His job is writing, and if they won't give him anything to write, he won't get paid."

"Hey, maybe that's the answer!" said Brendan. "We'll find him something to write."

"Yes," said Molly, "remember the time the Celtic brooch from the Ballygandon Hoard was stolen, and we tracked it down here. Your father got a great scoop out of that."

"A scoop of what?" Dessy asked.

"It's a newspaper word," said Brendan. "It means a big story for the paper that someone gets first."

"We've got one ready-made here," said Molly excitedly. "Princess Ethna's diary!"

"That would be great," said Brendan, "but we don't know yet whether that document *is* the diary."

"I'm sure it is," said Molly, "and as soon as it's definite, your father can be first with the story. We must let him know."

In the yard, as Locky was about to get into his car, Brendan and Molly told him about the exciting find in the library, without letting on that they had overheard the news about Brendan's father.

"It will make a really good story for the paper," Brendan said.

As Brendan had hoped, Locky was very interested. "That's right," he said, "just the sort of thing your father could do. I'll alert him that it's coming up. Then he can get in touch with your library and find out what's happening."

"I hope he'll get a better reception than we did today," said Molly.

"What do you mean?" Locky asked.

They told him about the arrival of Miss Carr and how snooty she had been to them.

"She sounds a bit of a pain, all right," said Locky, "but let's hope it's just first impressions.   She may not be as awful as she seemed."

But, as they were soon to discover, she was even worse.

3

Discoveries

When they went to the library a few days later, old Mrs O'Regan who ran the paper shop was at the counter, handing in a book.

"You realise this is overdue?" said Miss Carr, examining it.

"Oh no, I didn't, I'm sorry," said Mrs O'Regan.

"Three days overdue," said Miss Carr. "That will be fifteen pence."

"Oh dear," said Mrs O'Regan. "Joan Bright never used to charge. I just didn't notice . . ."

"Miss Bright was clearly not efficient," said Miss Carr. "But I'm running the library now, and I'll run it according to my rules."

"Very well," said Mrs O'Regan. "Here you are." She handed over the fifteen pence, and said: "I heard about Joan's mother. She's so good to her. When do you think she'll be back?"

"I have no idea," said Miss Carr. "She may not

come back at all. After all, she must be near retiring age."

Molly, Brendan and Dessy looked at one another, worried. This was the first they had heard about Miss Bright retiring and not coming back. Molly went past the counter into the main library and the others followed.

"And where are you three going, may I ask?" said Miss Carr.

"We were just going to look for some books to take out," said Molly.

"This being a library, you see . . ." said Dessy, smiling, as though he was explaining to an idiot.

"That's quite enough from *you*," said Miss Carr. "Well, be quick about it, and don't dawdle around or untidy the shelves."

Someone else came in just then, so Miss Carr was kept busy at the counter. The Ballygandon Gang went to the far end of the library where the Local History section was.

"Car-Wash is a real menace," said Brendan softly.

"And look," said Molly, "she seems to have taken away most of the chairs, and all the cushions. There's nowhere to sit around and read."

"I was looking at the notice-board while we waited," said Brendan. "She's taken down the notice about times for storytelling sessions. And there was one about a visiting author too. It's got *CANCELLED* scrawled over it."

"Hang on a minute," said Dessy, "I'll be right back." He went across to the Humour shelves, and came back again, saying: "There's no sign of Internet. I bet she's shut her down in the cellar."

"Let's have a look," said Brendan.

They crept across to the door that led to the basement, and opened it carefully. Molly turned on the light. They closed the door behind them and tiptoed slowly down the stairs. The basement seemed to be empty. Internet was nowhere to be seen.

"She's not even hiding under the stairs like she did before," said Dessy.

Molly called in a quiet voice: "Internet! Internet! Are you there?"

They heard a faint m*iaow*. "She's here!" said Brendan. "But I still can't see her."

There was another *miaow*.

"It came from over there, where the cupboard is," said Molly. They went across the room. The door of the cupboard in the alcove was slightly open. Brendan pulled it. Internet was crouched in the hole where the stones had been removed. Molly bent down and stroked her. Internet gave her usual yawn, then began to *miaow* again.

"We should have brought some cat-food," said Brendan.

"We will, next time," said Molly.

Dessy took a paper bag out of his pocket. "How about these?" he said. He opened the bag and took out some liquorice allsorts.

21

"I never heard of a cat eating liquorice allsorts," said Brendan.

Dessy said: "Haven't you heard people say, 'It takes *ALL SORTS* to make a world'?" He knelt down and held out his hand. Internet sniffed at the sweets, then began to munch one eagerly.

"She really must be hungry," said Molly. "The poor cat, fancy having to be shut up down here! We'll sneak in some proper food for her, and some water and a litter-tray. Car-Wash ought to be had up for cruelty to animals."

"Hey, we must be getting back," said Brendan, "before she finds out where we are."

They crept back up the stairs, leaving Internet the bag of sweets.

Luckily, Miss Carr was still busy at the counter, and they were able to browse among the shelves again. Molly took a book called *Twenty Famous Ghost Stories,* and they went to the counter.

"Mind you don't keep it beyond that date," said the librarian, stamping the book.

"I won't," said Molly. "Miss Carr, I was wondering if you'd heard anything yet from the history experts, the ones who were looking at the document from the basement?"

"Oh, you know about that, do you?" said Miss Carr. She sounded disapproving.

"Yes. Miss Bright told us."

"Did she indeed? I would have thought it was wiser

to wait to find out, before telling all and sundry. However, we have heard nothing yet. These experts can take forever. Anyway, we'll probably find out in the end that it's nothing important – maybe even a forgery."

Later that day, the Ballygandon Gang were wandering around the ruins of the castle on the hill. They almost felt they were like caretakers, making sure Princess Ethna's old home was preserved. There were sometimes vandals who came at night and wrote things on the walls, pushed down loose stones and left empty beer-cans and cider bottles lying around.

"I can just imagine Princess Ethna, up in that tower there, writing her diary," said Molly. "I wonder what she said."

"Supposing it's not the real thing, like Car-Wash thinks," said Brendan.

"I'm sure she's talking nonsense," said Molly. "She probably said that just to put us off."

"Yes, she didn't seem too pleased that we knew about the document at all," said Brendan.

"Perhaps she *has* heard, and didn't want to tell us," Dessy suggested.

"Maybe," said Molly. "We'll ask Miss Bright when we go and see her. Car-Wash would have to tell *her*."

"Unless she's planning her own exhibition, and doesn't want Joan Bright to get the credit," Brendan wondered.

"We could paint a slogan on the library," Dessy said. "CAR-WASH, COME CLEAN!"

"You'll be joining the vandals who come up here next," said Brendan. "Look at that." They had come to one of the outer walls of the castle. Someone had chalked the letters ED on it. Brendan picked up a tuft of grass and began to rub the letters out. Suddenly he gave a cry of shock.

"What's up?" asked Dessy.

"I felt the ground giving way under me," said Brendan. "There's a loose stone. Look!" He stepped away from the wall.

They could see a stone that had slipped and fallen, revealing a hollow in the wall.

"It looks like a small cave," said Dessy.

Molly said: "I'm going to take a closer look."

"Be careful," said Brendan. "I nearly fell when that stone gave way."

Molly went down the short slope towards the opening, step by step. She peered into the hollow. "I can't see much," she said.

"Take this," said Brendan, handing her his pocket torch.

"Thanks." Molly flashed the torch into the opening. "It certainly looks as if it has proper built-up stone walls, but it only goes in a couple of metres, then it's blocked up with big stones."

She scrambled back up the slope.

"What do you think it was for?" Brendan asked.

"It could have been a hiding-place," said Molly. "Someone could hole up there if there were people looking for them."

"Perhaps it was a place to hide away food and drink for emergencies," said Dessy.

"Like liquorice allsorts?" smiled Brendan.

"Whoever Ed is, he's a dimwit," said Molly, "scrawling his name there to make himself feel important."

Brendan went over to the wall and began rubbing out the letters. He stopped and said: "Suppose the letters weren't just someone scrawling his name? They might be showing where something was, a reminder, like."

"Buried treasure, do you mean?" asked Molly.

"Or showing where to find that hole in the wall. We didn't see it, remember, till that stone slipped."

"Who'd want a hiding-place like that, these days?" said Dessy.

"I don't know," said Brendan. "Next time we come we'll bring a spade, and see if we can find anything hidden behind those stones."

Suddenly Molly said: "Ssssh!"

"What's wrong?" Brendan whispered.

"Look over by the tower. I thought I saw someone peering out and then dodging back again out of sight."

"Who?" asked Dessy.

"I couldn't see."

"Perhaps it was Princess Ethna," said Dessy.

"Don't joke about her," said Molly. "Come on."

She started to move quietly across the grass and the tumbled stones that littered the ground, towards the tower. Brendan and Dessy followed. They reached the tower and listened. There was no sound except the whistling of the wind through the ruins, and the cawing of the crows perched up on the battlements.

Molly crept slowly round the side of the tower. There was no one to be seen.

"If there was anyone here, they've slipped away," she said. "I guess they didn't want us to see them."

"What's that noise?" asked Brendan. "Over there, on the other side of the wall." He ran across to the castle wall and looked through a gap where there had once been a window. *"Look, down there!"* he cried.

The others ran across to look.

"There's someone running down the hill," said Brendan. "She looks familiar."

The figure was zig-zagging down the steep slope, stumbling now and then on the rough ground. It was a woman with long black hair. She looked back to see if she had been seen, but she obviously didn't notice the three watchers behind the wall.

"She's familiar all right," said Molly. "Her hair's different, but I know that face. Remember Dervla, Seamus Gallagher's daughter? The one that gave us all the hassle with the fake ancestor-tracing, and messing about with the graves? That's *her!*"

26

4

Messages in Code

Dervla was indeed a trouble-maker, not at all bothered if something she did was against the law. Her father Seamus had a pub in the town nearby. They'd run a scheme where Dervla in California had found rich Americans seeking their roots, and Seamus had changed the names on the graves in a churchyard to match them.

The Ballygandon Gang had found them out, and they had both been arrested.

But while she was out on bail, Dervla had disappeared, leaving her father to face a huge fine for fraud. She had never been heard of since.

"Dervla!" said Brendan. "She's got a nerve, showing her face around here. If the Guards see her, they'll put her in jail."

"She must be on to some other very big scheme, to risk coming back," said Molly.

"Very big, and very dodgy, most likely," said Dessy.

"What was she doing up here in the Castle?" Brendan wondered.

"Maybe it had something to do with that hole in the wall you found." Molly went back across the rough ground to the wall. She looked at the hole. "Perhaps she was going to hide something there, and we disturbed her," she said.

"Listen," said Brendan. "Let's put the stone back so that it hides the entrance again. Then I'll finish rubbing out the letters. If she comes back looking for the hiding-place, she won't know where it is."

"That's a nutty idea," said Dessy. "We won't know where it is either, if *we* want to find it."

"Dessy's right," said Molly. "Let's leave what's left of the letters."

"OK," said Brendan, "but if you ever call my ideas nutty again, Dessy, I'm going to push your head into the hole and leave it there."

Dessy opened his mouth to reply, but Molly said: "Stay calm, boys! No squabbling. We can't have the Ballygandon Gang falling out with each other."

Brendan grunted, and Dessy shrugged. They set to work putting back the stone.

Next day they went to the library again. Molly had her satchel with her, containing two books, two plastic bowls, a plastic bottle of water, and a packet of cat-food – the dry kind that looks like a breakfast cereal. That way there wouldn't be any smell which might drift upstairs into the library and alert Miss Carr.

"You're back already, are you?" said Miss Carr, taking the ghost story book which Molly handed her.

"I'm a quick reader," said Molly. "Besides, that book didn't have the best ghost story of all."

"And which one is that?" asked Miss Carr without interest.

"Oh, the story of Princess Ethna. You know that one, don't you, Miss Carr? She was due to be married to a Prince from another clan, and the night before the wedding, up there in the Castle, she was found murdered, stabbed by a Celtic brooch . . ."

Miss Carr was frowning. "Fantasy, pure fantasy," she said, "just like the diary."

"The diary?" asked Brendan, "The one that was found here?"

"Have you heard from the people in Dublin about it?" Molly asked eagerly.

"What?" Miss Carr said sharply. "Oh, the people in Dublin . . ." She sounded flustered, as though she hadn't meant to mention the diary. Then she said: "It's none of your business, but to stop you going on about it, I might as well tell you that I *have* heard from the people in Dublin."

"Great!" said Brendan.

"Not at all great," said Miss Carr. "That document is worthless. It's just some old pieces of paper which someone has scrawled on. It's not even a diary, as it turns out."

"Will they send the papers back here?" asked Molly.

"There's no point," said Miss Carr, "since they're not of any interest. Now, are you going to choose another book? I have work to do."

"Yes, I'll just go and find one," said Molly. They went to the far side of the library. Making sure Miss Carr wasn't looking, they quietly opened the door and crept down the stairs to the basement.

Molly opened her satchel and took out the bowls. *"Puss, puss, puss!"* She called softly. "Where are you, Internet? It's dinner-time!" She opened the bag and tipped some of the cat-food into the bowl. Dessy poured some water from the bottle into the other bowl.

They looked around the basement. The cat was nowhere to be seen.

"I expect she's in the cupboard again," said Brendan, going across and opening the door. The cupboard was empty. Brendan looked down into the shallow hole in the bottom. "She's definitely not in here," he said, closing the door again.

They checked under the stairs and on the shelves. There was no sign of Internet anywhere.

"The Case of the Vanishing Cat!" said Dessy.

"Seriously, where can she have got to?" wondered Brendan.

"Maybe Car-Wash left the door open and she sneaked out," said Dessy.

Molly said suddenly: "Oh, no!"

"What's the matter?" asked Brendan.

"I've just thought – you don't suppose Car-Wash has got rid of her? Taken her to the vet and . . ." Molly was almost tearful.

"We'll soon find out!" Brendan said angrily. He strode towards the stairs. Just then they heard a *miaow,* then another.

"She's here!" cried Molly in relief.

"It came from the cupboard," said Dessy, going across and opening the door.

Internet came out and looked around calmly. Molly rushed over and picked her up and stroked her.

"Oh, Internet," she said, "we thought we'd lost you!" She put the cat down beside the bowl and it began to gobble away at the food.

"I just can't understand it," said Brendan. "That cupboard was empty just now, and suddenly there's the cat, inside it!" He went over and opened the door again. He knelt down and felt along the wall at the back. "This is it!" he cried.

"What's what?" asked Dessy, peering over Brendan's shoulder.

"See there," said Brendan. "There's a stone sticking out from the side, and behind it there's a hole. Internet must have gone in there. Maybe she finds it a snug place to sleep."

"Well, we'll know where to look, next time," said Molly.

Reluctantly, they left Internet munching happily at

her food, and went back into the library. Molly took a book called *Haunted Castles* from the shelf, and they moved over to the counter. No one was there.

"Where's Car-Wash gone?" asked Brendan.

"Sssh! She'll hear you!" Molly warned.

They peered round the bookstacks, but there was no one around.

"The Case of the Vanishing Librarian!" said Dessy.

Brendan glanced into the office, but there was no one there either.

He came back to the counter. Dessy was smiling. He had his hands behind his back. "Hey, Brendan, do you like dates?" he asked.

"I do," said Brendan.

"You're in luck," said Dessy. "Shut your eyes and hold out your hand."

"This is some kind of a cod," said Brendan.

"You'll never know till you try," said Dessy.

"OK, Dessy," Brendan sighed. He put his hand, palm up, on the counter, and shut his eyes.

"There!" said Dessy, quickly producing the rubber library date-stamp from behind his back, and bringing it down on Brendan's palm. "A date in your hand!"

Brendan looked down. There on his hand was the date in purple letters.

"You fooled me there, Dessy," said Brendan, laughing. Molly laughed too.

"How does that work?" asked Brendan.

"Simple," said Dessy, showing him the stamp.

"There's a row of rubber ribbons and you just roll them round to the right date and then stamp the yoke on this ink-pad."

"Oh, you mean, like this?" said Brendan. He seized the date-stamp and planted it fairly and squarely on Dessy's forehead.

"Now nobody will be able to say you don't know what day it is," said Brendan. "It's written all over your face!"

"OK, you win," said Dessy. "Hey, maybe we've invented a new kind of tattoo! We could set up a stall at the market: 'GET UP TO DATE WITH DESSY'S TATTOO CALENDAR!'"

"Where can Car-Wash have got to?" said Molly.

"What about the Computer Room?" Brendan suggested. They went towards it. The door was closed, but they could hear movement inside. Brendan opened the door. Miss Carr was in there, fiddling with the plugs behind the computer. She looked up, startled.

"What do you want?" she snapped.

"I'd like to take out this book," said Molly.

"Right, I'll be with you in a minute," said Miss Carr.

"Do you want any help with that?" asked Dessy. "Brendan is quite a whizz-kid at computers."

"Is he really?" said Miss Carr coldly. "Well, he won't be able to use his skills here. I don't think there's any place for computers in a library. Books are what we're about, not electronic mumbo-jumbo. I'm going to sell off this machine and buy more books with the money." She turned back to the plugs. She had just pulled out the printer plug when the telephone rang, out in the library.

Miss Carr left the room, saying: "Touch nothing. I'll be back in a moment."

"She's dismantling the whole place," said Brendan. "Maybe she'll even decide to sell off the books."

"I wonder if she's telling the truth about the document?" said Molly. "Perhaps the experts haven't said it's worth nothing. Perhaps it really is Princess Ethna's diary!"

"How can we find out?" asked Dessy.

There was a bleeping sound from the computer. They looked at the screen. A string of letters began to appear on it.

"What's happening?" said Brendan. "Did you touch the keyboard?"

"Not me," said Molly.

"Neither did I," Dessy said. They looked at the screen. A message was on it, flashing. It began:

TO: MBD

HELP!

"How did that get there?" Brendan asked.

"There's more," said Molly, as another string of letters appeared. They looked at them, puzzled. It was just a jumble of letters without meaning:

EQHDMCR – RZUD LX VNQCR

"There must be some fault in the machine," said Dessy. "That's just gobbledy-gook."

"Perhaps it's some kind of code," said Brendan. "I'll write it down, in case we can work it out later." He took out his notebook and wrote down the letters. He was only just in time.

Miss Carr came back into the room. "What are you doing?" she asked. "What's that you're writing on the screen?"

As she spoke, the screen went blank.

"We didn't touch it," said Molly. "It was just switching itself off, I suppose."

"Well, I'm going to switch it off for good, as far as the library is concerned." Miss Carr pulled the plugs out of their sockets. "There!" she said with satisfaction. "Now I'll just check your book out, and then you can be off."

The kitchen table at Molly's house was covered in pieces of paper, full of scrawled letters and crossings out. The heads of the Ballygandon Gang were bent over the table, trying to work out what the message on the screen could mean.

"The only clear word is HELP," said Brendan. We don't even know what MBD means."

"Maybe it's a name or some initials, like ED on the castle wall," said Dessy. "That's it!" said Molly. "M – B – D. They're *our* initials! Molly, Brendan, Dessy. It's a message to us!"

"But who from?" asked Dessy. "And what does it mean?"

"We've got to crack the code." said Brendan. "Maybe we've been trying too complicated answers. The simplest codes just play around with the alphabet. Like putting the letter that comes before the real letter, each time. Let's try it. The coded message starts EQHDMCR. Now, the letter before E is D, the one before Q is P, the one before H is G......" He began writing down the letters. After a while, he looked at the decoding:

DPGCLBQ – QYTC KW ....

He stopped. "It still doesn't mean anything," he said. "Suppose we try the letter *after* each letter in the code . . . First letter E, so we put F, next letter Q, so we put R, third letter H, put I, then D, so we put E, then M, put N . . ." Then he said excitedly: "Yes! It's making sense. Look, the first word is FRIENDS!"

"Great work, Brendan!" said Dessy.

Brendan went on translating the other letters. Finally he said: "There it is!"

They all stared down at the message he had written out:

FRIENDS – SAVE MY WORDS

"I still don't know what it means," said Dessy.

"What words do we have to save?" Brendan asked.

Molly looked very serious. She said: "Perhaps the words that were found in the document in the basement. The words in Princess Ethna's diary . . ."

5

Computer Capers

"But who sent the message to the computer?" Dessy asked.

"Well, it does say SAVE *MY* WORDS . . ." said Molly, "and it's the diary that needs to be saved."

"Wow!" said Brendan, "do you really think it was sent by Princess Ethna, or her spirit or whatever?"

"It does sound fantastic," said Molly, "but strange things have happened around here before. Things no one can explain."

"Come off it!" said Dessy. "That's not possible. It's somebody trying to cod us."

"Who?" said Molly. "Miss Carr wouldn't be sending us coded messages, and she's the only one who could have got at the computer."

"It's weird," said Brendan.

"Out of this world," said Dessy.

"Exactly," said Molly. "Look, it sounds far-fetched and weird all right, but I think we've got to act as if

37

that's the explanation. And that means Miss Carr is lying about the document being worth nothing. She must have heard from the experts and not told anyone."

"So if that *is* the diary, where is it?" asked Brendan.

"My guess is that she's got it back, and is keeping it quiet."

"But why?" Dessy wondered.

"Maybe she's planning to sell it secretly," said Molly. "and if she is, she must have hidden it somewhere."

"Hey!" Brendan said excitedly, "maybe it was in that hollow in the castle wall, the one we found with the loose stone over it."

"And perhaps ED stands for *Ethna's Diary!*" cried Molly.

"Well, if it does, it's not there now, for sure," said Dessy. "The hole was empty."

"I've got it!" said Molly. "Dervla Gallagher! That's what she was doing at the castle – taking away the diary. She must be in league with Miss Carr."

"So where will they hide it now?" Brendan wondered.

"Probably in the library, where she can get at it easily," said Molly.

"We'll have to hunt for them," said Brendan.

"It's going to be hard to do it without making Car-Wash suspicious," said Dessy.

"Let's have a look at night when the library is closed," said Molly.

"How would we get in?" said Dessy.

"We'll think of something," said Brendan optimistically.

"Hey, I've just thought of something else!" said Molly. "We've got to act fast."

"What's up?" said Dessy.

"The computer!" Molly exclaimed. "Supposing there are more messages for us? If Car-Wash sells the computer, we'll never get them."

Just then her grandfather, Locky, came into the room. "Hello there!" he said. "How's the Ballygandon Gang?"

"Fine, Grandpa," said Molly. She looked at Brendan and Dessy, and gave a slight shake of her head. She meant that they shouldn't tell Locky about the message and the diary just yet.

Locky saw the sheets of paper and the jumble of letters written on them. "What's this? Word-games?" he asked.

"Yes, we were just practising some codes," said Brendan.

Molly had an idea. "Grandpa," she said. "You know what you need where you live, at Horseshoe House? A computer!"

Locky laughed. "A computer? There's one in the office already, I don't think Mrs Boyd would need another one."

"Not for the office, Grandpa," Molly said. "For you and the other residents."

"What would we do with a computer? We wouldn't know one end of it from the other."

"They're not hard to work," said Brendan. "and you could do your betting calculations on it, for the horse-races."

"Really?" Locky was definitely interested. "Well, if it would help me work out the racing form . . ."

"Oh, it would, Grandpa," said Brendan. "It's really scientific."

"And you could play games on it too," said Dessy.

"Come to think of it," said Locky, "those two McDonald sisters are always playing cards. Maybe there are games *they* could play on it. It might keep them from quarrelling with each other all the time."

"There are lots of programs with card-games you can get," said Brendan.

"Well, I'll think about it, certainly," said Locky.

"The thing is, Grandpa," said Molly, "there's a good second-hand computer being sold by the woman in the library."

"Car-Wash," said Dessy.

"The woman in the car-wash?" Locky was confused.

"No, the library," said Molly. "She's called Miss Carr, and she's selling the computer. It's a perfectly good one, it's just that she doesn't approve of computers in libraries for some reason."

"Well, I'll call round and see her some time," said Locky.

"How about now?" said Brendan. "It might be sold if we're not quick about it."

It wasn't hard to persuade Locky. They drove from the house up to the library in his car, and Molly introduced him to Miss Carr. She took him to the computer room and Locky examined the machine, pretending that he knew something about it. The Ballygandon Gang hung around outside the open door.

Then Locky said: "And what sort of price were you thinking of asking for it?"

"I thought two hundred and fifty pounds would be fair," said Miss Carr.

Locky loved to bargain. "Let's call it two hundred," he said.

"Two hundred and twenty," said Miss Carr.

"It's a deal!" said Locky. "I've got my cheque-book here."

As he was reaching into his pocket, Miss Carr said: "I'd really prefer cash, if you don't mind."

Locky was surprised, but he said: "I don't mind. As it happens, I've just collected some big winnings from my bet on Saturday's race."

He reached into his pocket and produced a bulging wallet. Molly and the others watched wide-eyed as he took out the notes and handed them to Miss Carr.

"Thank you," she said. "I'll put this in the library safe right away."

Brendan and Dessy joined Locky in the computer room. At the door Molly turned and glanced back at Miss Carr. She saw her go towards the office, but she stopped behind the counter near the main door. She glanced around furtively, and then picked up her handbag and quickly stuffed the money into it.

Molly went in to help the others. Soon Miss Carr was back to watch the small procession coming out of the computer room. Brendan and Dessy carried the computer, Molly followed with the printer, and Locky at the end carried a bunch of plugs and wires.

"I hope you've got everything," said Miss Carr.

"No problem," said Locky. "We'll all be high-tech wizards at Horseshoe House before long."

Locky opened the boot of the car. Inside there was a jumble of oil-cans, spanners, old racing magazines and papers, and a couple of bundled-up rugs. Brendan cleared a space and spread the papers on the floor of the boot, and put the rugs on top of them.

"We'll lay it on those," he said, "we don't want anything to be damaged by the jolting of Locky's car."

"Jolting?" said Locky indignantly. "I'll have you know, this car is state-of-the-art!"

"State-of-the-scrapyard, more like," Brendan whispered to Dessy as they loaded the gear into the boot. Finally Locky slammed it shut and they all got into the car.

"Listen while I tell you what I saw," said Molly as Locky put the key in the dashboard. He paused and turned round to hear what Molly had to say. Molly told them about Miss Carr and where she had put the money.

"It doesn't look as if that money will be buying many books for the library," said Dessy.

"I thought it was odd when she asked for it in cash," said Locky, starting the engine. "But we can't prove she's spending it on herself instead of on the library. Now it's time I was getting back to Horseshoe House with all those high-tech goodies."

"Hey," said Dessy. "How about this one? What does one computer say when it meets another one?"

"Tell us, Dessy," said Brendan.

"Hi, Tech!" Dessy cried, making a high-five gesture.

"You're a riot," said Brendan.

"I'll drop our stand-up comic friend and the rest of you at your house, Molly," said Locky. "I can't wait to impress the folks at Horseshoe House with my computer skills."

"But Grandpa, you've never used a computer, have you?" said Molly.

"You're never too old to learn," said Locky.

"I've got an idea," said Brendan, "why don't we come with you and help you set it up?"

Locky was delighted. "We'll call in and tell your mother we're off to Horseshoe Cyber-House," he said.

There was great excitement among the residents when Locky announced his latest purchase. Mrs Boyd suggested they set up the machine in the corner of the large living-room, where there was a small table.

As Brendan, Molly and Dessy plugged up the machine, Locky told the group of residents watching with interest: "There's nothing to it, you know, once you get the knack of these gadgets. You'll soon find it as easy as turning on the toaster."

"Brenda can't even work that without burning the toast," said Harriet McDonald.

"It was only the once," said Brenda, "and that was because you called me over to pour your tea for you."

"Nonsense," said her sister.

"Now, now, ladies," said Locky. "enough of this bickering, or you won't be let at the computer for your card-games. The machine will seize up."

"There!" said Brendan, triumphantly. "It's all systems go!"

Everyone watched as the screen lit up and the machine went through its switching-on routine.

"Bravo, the Ballygandon Gang!" said Locky, clapping his hands. The other residents joined in. Brendan, Molly and Dessy raised their fists in the air.

"What's it saying now?" asked Harriet McDonald, pointing at the screen.

They all looked. A string of letters had appeared on the screen:

KNNJ HM BDKKZQ

Brendan whispered to Molly: "I bet it's another coded message. We mustn't let on. I'll write it down while you chat."

Molly said: "It's just a bit of a hiccup in the switching-on system. You sometimes get these bugs creeping in at first. It's not a problem, we'll just do a re-start." She looked at Brendan who was hunched over, writing secretly in his notebook.

He closed the book and nodded. "Got it," he whispered.

Molly went to the machine and pressed a few keys. There was a whirring sound from the computer, then the screen went blank. It immediately lit up again and the switch-on routine began again. There was another round of applause. Molly thought the elderly residents of Horseshoe House looked like children round a Christmas tree.

"When can we start the card-game?" asked Brenda McDonald.

"We'll have to get you some software for that, and for the racing calculations," said Brendan. "We'll bring it as soon as we can. Meanwhile, you can write things on the machine, and print them out."

"I'll show you," said Mrs Boyd, who ran Horseshoe House.

"Meanwhile, I'll take my gang back to Ballygandon," said Locky.

When they got into the car, he took some notes from his wallet and gave them to Brendan. "You'll need this to buy that soft stuff for the machine."

"Software, Grandpa," said Molly. "It's just the disks which run the programs."

"That's what I meant," said Locky, totally bewildered.

As they drove back to Ballygandon, Brendan said to Locky, trying to sound casual: "Grandpa, if any of those jumbled letters like the last ones come on the screen again, would you write them down for us and let us know what they are? It's quite often a message showing something has to be put right with the machine."

"No problem," said Locky.

Back at Molly's house, Brendan, Molly and Dessy sat on the fence of the yard outside the shop. Brendan had his notebook open.

"It must have been another message," said Brendan. He looked at the letters he'd copied down:

KNNJ HM BDKKZQ.

"This stuff is making me shiver," said Dessy

"Me too," said Molly. "But we've got to go with it."

"If the code's the same as before," said Brendan, writing. Then K stands for L, and N stands for O and N for another O, and then J becomes K.... We're right! That's the first word!   LOOK."

"We *are* looking," said Dessy.

"I mean LOOK is the word," said Brendan. "Now let's do the rest." He scribbled in his notebook as he decoded the letters.   Then he said: "That's it!"

Molly looked at the words he had written: "LOOK IN CELLAR," she said.

"Now we've only got to find the right cellar," said Dessy.

"It must mean the basement of the library, where the diary was first found," said Molly. "Car-Wash has definitely hidden it there."

"But we searched all around in there, when we were looking for Internet," said Brendan.

"There must be a secret hiding-place somewhere," Molly said. "But we'll need time to look for it."

"We've got to get in when the library's closed and Car-Wash has gone," said Dessy.

"But how?" Brendan asked. "We can't break down the door, and the windows are too high up to get to, without someone seeing us climbing up there."

"I could ask my brother to come down if you like," said Dessy doubtfully. "he's done a bit of burglary in his time."

"And done time in prison for it," said Brendan. "I don't think that's a good idea. We might all end up inside."

"That's the answer!" Molly exclaimed. "We've got to be inside! One of us must be inside the library, when it closes. We'll go in there just before closing-time, and I'll hide in the basement. With any luck, Car-Wash won't notice. Then after it gets dark, you come back and I'll open the door to you. We'll all go down to the basement and do a really thorough search."

"It's a good plan," said Brendan. "When shall we do it?"

"There's no time to lose," said Molly. "Why not this evening?"

6

Night Search

Miss Carr was not in the main part of the library when they arrived.

"She must be in the office," said Brendan.

"Counting her cash, I expect," said Dessy.

"This is our chance," said Molly. "I'll go down into the basement right away, and wait there. The library will be closing in half an hour, and it will start to get dark about half an hour after that. I'll be expecting you."

"We'd better give you a signal when we're outside the door," said Brendan.

"I could yodel, if you like," said Dessy.

"And have the whole street looking out to tell you to shut up?" Molly said.

"Oh come on, it's not that bad," said Dessy. "Listen to this . . ." But Brendan clamped his hand over Dessy's mouth before he could give voice.

"I know," said Molly. "Brendan can give his owl hoot imitation, softly. I'll be waiting near the door."

"OK," said Brendan. "Here, you'd better take my torch. You can't risk leaving the light on."

Molly took it. She gave them the thumbs-up sign and then went between the bookstacks to the far end of the library. She opened the basement door and went in.

She was just in time. The office door opened and Miss Carr came out. She didn't look very pleased to see them. "Well, it's you again!" she said.

"Yes, Miss Carr," Brendan said politely. "We just came to thank you for the computer you sold to my grandfather. It's up and running in the place he lives, Horseshoe House. I'm sure they'll all get great value from it."

"I hope so," said Miss Carr. "Now if you're going to get any books out, you'd better be quick about it. We're closing soon." She looked at her watch.

"It's OK, we're just going," said Brendan.

"Is the girl with you?" Miss Carr looked around the library.

"No, Molly had to do some messages," said Brendan. "Well, we'll be off now. Thanks again for the computer."

"I hope Molly will be all right," said Dessy, as he and Brendan walked up the road.

"I'm sure she will," said Brendan. They decided to walk up to the castle to pass the time before they could call back to the library.

They looked at the place where they had found the

hole in the wall. The stone covering it was still in place. "Let's take a look," said Brendan. Together they lifted away the stone. The hollow in the wall was empty, just as it had been before.

"What's that?" said Dessy suddenly. He bent down, close to the place where the stone floor joined the wall. "There seem to be some scratches on the stone," he said.

"Maybe it happened when they were getting the hidden diary out," said Brendan. "Or perhaps it comes from the time of Princess Ethna," said Dessy in a ghost-story kind of voice. "I bet a prisoner was walled up here and tried to scratch his way out before he died a horrible death inside!"

"Stop acting the eejit," said Brendan. But he still felt a bit uneasy.

"Hey, I heard something!" Dessy cried.

"Stop joking," said Brendan.

"It's true," said Dessy. "A clicking sound, over by the tower."

"Get down!" said Brendan. They both crouched down in the hollow in the wall, hoping they wouldn't be spotted. From behind the tower, camera in hand, came the figure they had seen running down the hill the other day. This time they had no doubts: it was definitely Dervla Gallagher. When they had last seen her in California and again back in Ireland, she had smartly styled bronze-coloured hair. Now it was jet black, and long, falling round her shoulders.

"That's probably a wig she's wearing," Brendan whispered. "But I'd know that face anywhere. She looks as cunning as ever."

"I don't think she saw us," said Dessy, peering out. "I wonder what she's up to."

They watched Dervla walking around the castle courtyard, photographing the tower from various angles.

"You can bet it isn't for her photograph album," said Brendan. "It must be some other scam, like the ancestor-tracing."

"That's Princess Ethna's tower," said Dessy. "Do you think it's something to do with the diary?"

"Dessy, you could be right," said Brendan. "I hope she gets a move on, or we'll be late getting to the library."

Molly was sitting on the top step of the basement stairs, with Internet the cat on her lap, purring loudly. She heard Miss Carr moving around in the library, tidying up. Then she heard the main door slammed shut.

The basement was very dark. Molly switched on Brendan's torch and flashed it around. She wouldn't want to spend too long here, she thought. She listened with her ear to the door. The library was silent. She pushed the door ajar. It was still light outside.

"I'll be right back, Internet," she told the cat, putting her down on the stairs and slipping out of the door into the library. The empty silence was eerie. Molly would have liked to play her tin whistle, just to break

51

the mood, but she was afraid it would be heard out in the road.

She opened the door of the computer room and looked at the empty desk. At least Miss Carr's greed for money had meant that Locky and his friends at Horseshoe House had a computer to entertain them. She wondered if there were any more messages. If only the computer was still here, then whoever or whatever it might be, could get in touch with them.

Then she nearly jumped in the air with shock, as she heard a thudding sound out in the library. She hardly dared to leave the computer room, but she forced herself to go out. She tiptoed round among the bookstacks. Nothing seemed to have been disturbed. Then she noticed a book lying on the floor, in the Local History section near the basement door.

She was sure it hadn't been there before. She went over and picked it up. It was called *Dungeon Days*. She flicked through the pages. They were full of accounts of people who had been imprisoned in the old days, centuries ago.

Was it just a coincidence that it had fallen off the shelf? Or was this another mysterious event like the ones Miss Bright had told them about? Molly put the book back. It was beginning to get quite dark now. She went towards the main door, ready to let Brendan and Dessy in.

As she waited, it got darker and darker. Molly didn't like to switch on the torch. She listened. The air seemed to be full of strange whispering sounds – it must be the wind blowing through cracks in the windows. She shivered. Was it getting cold, or was she just feeling scared? Where were Brendan and Dessy?

Just then, she heard a faint sound like an owl hooting. It was Brendan's signal. Molly opened the door, and Brendan and Dessy slipped in.

"Sorry, we were held up," said Brendan.

"And wait till you hear why," said Dessy. They told Molly how they had seen Dervla in the castle, taking photographs of the tower.

"Do you think it could have anything to do with Miss Carr and the diary?" said Brendan.

"I wouldn't be surprised," said Molly. "If we can only find the diary, we can soon find out. Let's get searching!"

They could just see enough to find their way past the bookstacks to the basement door. Molly told them about the book that had fallen off the shelf.

"This gets weirder by the minute," said Dessy.

Molly opened the door. There was a screech as Internet, surprised, jumped off the top step and ran down the stairs.

"Can we risk turning on the light?" Brendan wondered.

"We'll have to, I reckon," said Molly, "we won't be able to see enough with just a torch."

They went in and closed the door quickly behind them. They went down the stairs. Dessy produced a bag of cat-food and put it down for Internet, who began to gobble it eagerly.

"Let's take a wall each," said Brendan. "Search every nook and cranny, in case there's a hidden hole."

"There are four walls," said Dessy. "And those alcoves besides."

"I know that," said Brendan. "Let's call the cupboard wall A, the left-hand wall B, and the right-hand wall C, and the back wall D, and the alcoves E. So I'll do A, Molly B, and Dessy C, then we'll all confer, and tackle D and the alcoves together."

"Aye, aye, Captain," said Dessy.

"You can mock all you like, Dessy," said Brendan, "but we've got to have a proper plan."

"I agree," said Molly. "Let's go!"

After ten minutes, Brendan said: "OK, let's confer!"

They gathered in the centre of the basement room. Internet snaked around their legs, wanting to be stroked. Molly picked her up.

"Internet should be in on this, too," she said. "After all, she lives here."

Molly said she had examined the wall behind the stairs, and looked under the stairs too. There seemed to be nothing odd. Dessy had looked on the shelves, and opened the three or four boxes. Two were empty, and the others just contained old library records of books taken out, over the years.

Brendan said: "I had a good look in that cupboard where Internet was. It's totally empty. And that hole at the back where Internet was hiding. I flashed the torch in there, but I couldn't see anything. Maybe we should see if we can reach into it."

"It seems like the only possibility," said Molly. They went across to the cupboard and opened the door wide. They knelt down. Brendan reached into the hole at the back.

"I can't feel anything," he said.

"There's a piece of wood over there," said Molly. She went and got it and gave it to Brendan. He poked it into the hole.

"It's touching something," he said. "The trouble is, whatever it is, it's pushing it further in."

"I know the answer!" said Dessy. "Chewing gum!" He fished in his pocket and took out a packet. He put three pieces in his mouth and chewed heavily. Then he pulled out the squishy gum and offered it to Brendan.

Brendan looked at it with disgust. "Why don't *you* do it, Dessy?" he suggested.

"OK," said Dessy. "It's just an idea." He took the piece of wood and stuck the mushy gum on to the end of it. Then he knelt down and poked the wood into the hole. He groped around, then said: "I think it's stuck!" Slowly he began to pull the piece of wood out.

As it came out, they saw that there was a long cardboard tube with a metal lid, coming out with it. The tube was just emerging from the hole, when they all stopped and froze. Above in the library, they heard voices.

"Pull it out, Dessy!" cried Brendan.

Dessy pushed and pulled, but the gum came away from the tube when it was still inside the hole. They heard someone turning the handle of the basement door.

"Quick, get into the alcove!" cried Molly. She snatched up Internet and they rushed under the archway into the shallow alcove. Luckily the shadow from the light hid them. They wouldn't be seen unless someone was deliberately searching. But they could see the cupboard. Brendan had pushed the door closed as they scurried away.

They heard voices at the top of the basement stairs.

"That's odd, I thought I'd turned off this light." It was Miss Carr.

Then they heard another voice they knew, reply: "You're getting forgetful, Evanna. I hope you haven't forgotten where you put the diary."

They held their breath and looked at one another. They knew that voice too. It was Dervla Gallagher.

7

The Hiding Place

"The papers are well-hidden, I made sure of that," said Miss Carr. "And believe me, I am *not* getting forgetful. I just hope that some people are."

"What do you mean?" asked Dervla sharply.

"I mean the people round here, who might recognise you. Let's hope they are willing to forget your past activities. I am afraid the Guards won't."

"That's why I've got this black wig," said Dervla. "No one will know me. Anyway, I'm lying low at my father's place. Everyone thinks I'm out of the country."

"I'm surprised your father is even talking to you, after you left him in the lurch last time," said Miss Carr.

"I promised him a cut of this little scheme," said Dervla. "Now, where's the diary?"

The Ballygandon Gang watched from their hiding place in the shadows, as Miss Carr went across to the cupboard and opened it. She knelt down in front of it, and from her handbag produced what looked like some short lengths of piping.

"What's that?" asked Dervla.

"A folding walking-stick. Watch this." She held out the stick, and the sections, which were linked inside by strong elastic, flicked out to make a sturdy metal stick. *"Abracadabra!"* she cried.

Dessy whispered: "Hey, I could use that in my conjuring act."

Brendan frowned, and put his finger to his lips.

"I've stuck a magnet to the end," said Miss Carr, "so when we push the stick into this hole at the back of the cupboard . . ." She pushed the stick in, and pulled it out slowly. The metal top of the tube stuck to the magnet, and the entire tube came out. Miss Carr grasped it and stood up, saying: "Out comes the hidden treasure!"

"Let's have a look," said Dervla eagerly, reaching for the tube.

"All in good time," said Miss Carr. She carefully took the lid off the top of the tube and reached her fingers in. She slowly pulled out something that looked like a square of rolled up leather. She gave Dervla the empty tube to hold, and flattened the leather out. They could see that the leather was the cover of a book, and when Miss Carr opened it they saw pages that were old and yellow, like parchment. She held it out so that Dervla could read it.

"What's that?" asked Dervla. "I can't understand a word of it."

"It's written in Old Irish, that's why. I can only just work it out myself," said Miss Carr.

"Is that so?" said Dervla, unbelieving.

"Yes, I studied the language, you see," said Miss Carr. "Fortunately the experts in Dublin translated it. Here, take a look." She took some ordinary pages from the back of the parchment ones and handed them to Dervla.

Dervla began to read. "As I look out from this tower on the countryside below, I think of my coming wedding. My dear Fergal will one day be lord of all these lands . . ."

Miss Carr said: "Princess Ethna had come to marry Fergal, the son of the castle family, bringing a huge hoard of treasure as a dowry. But the night before the wedding, she was murdered in that very tower . . ."

"I know the story," said Dervla impatiently. "Sure, wasn't I up there photographing that tower for our publicity leaflet? It will really tempt the punters to see the actual place where it happened."

"Yes, well, we must take this upstairs and start preparing it. We'll make extracts from the diary to put in the leaflet too," said Miss Carr.

"Are we going back to your place?" asked Dervla.

"No, we'll sort it out up in the office. I don't want to risk taking the papers out of the library until we're quite ready for the trip. They'll be totally safe in the cupboard here."

"I've got the advance publicity organised," said Dervla.

"I hope you kept it discreet," said Miss Carr.

"Of course I did, just as we agreed. Only the really top collectors will know about the sale. People who will bid fantastic money for stuff like that."

"Good," said Miss Carr. "Let's get on with it, shall we?"

They had just started to go up the stairs, when Internet gave a *miaow*.

"What was that?" said Dervla.

"What?"

"I thought I heard a cat. I'm going to take a look."

She came back down the stairs and was coming towards the alcove, when Miss Carr said: "Don't worry. There's a cat that lives down here. I kicked it out of the library."

"I can't see it," said Dervla, peering about. Brendan, Molly and Dessy shrank back into the shadows.

Miss Carr said impatiently : "It lurks in the corners, looking for rats and mice I suppose. Do hurry up, Dervla! Come on!"

Dervla turned and followed Miss Carr up the stairs. The door shut behind them and the light went off.

Molly flashed the torch around as they came out of the alcove. She put the cat down, saying: "You almost gave us away then, Internet!" She stroked the cat, and it purred happily.

"Do you think she was right about the rats?" asked Dessy.

"Let's hope not," said Brendan.

"What shall we do now?" asked Dessy.

"Let's wait here till Car-Wash hides the diary again, and then we can take it," said Brendan.

"But they could be hours working on it," said Molly. "I said we'd be back. My mother will send out a search party if we're very late. We'll have to go."

"They'll see us if we go up into the library," said Dessy.

"They said they were going to work in the office," said Molly. "With any luck they'll have the door closed, and we can creep by and let ourselves out the main door."

"Goodbye, Internet," said Dessy. "Watch out for Mister Rat!"

When they were up in the library, Molly held the torch down low to shine on the floor, and they crept between the bookstacks till they could see the door of the office. They were in luck. The door was closed. They could just hear the voices of Car-Wash and Dervla inside.

"Now's our chance," said Molly. She led the way towards the main door, crouching down. The others followed. Very carefully, she turned the handle and opened the door. She looked out. There was no one around.

Soon they were out of the library and hurrying away down the road towards home.

Molly's parents were surprised when she offered to clear up after tea. They gladly went into the living-room to watch television.

"Come on, it won't take long," Molly said, as Brendan and Dessy began reluctantly to clear up. "I wanted us to be on our own, so that we could have a Council of War."

With the kitchen table cleared, they sat round it, planning what to do.

"We could tell the Guards," said Brendan. "After all, what Car-Wash is doing is out-and-out robbery."

"Why would they believe us, when we've got no proof?" said Dessy. "My brother always says, 'As long as there's no evidence, you're in the clear, boy!'"

Molly didn't think Dessy's criminal brother was the right kind of adviser, but it was true that without any evidence, there was no reason why the Guards would believe them, rather than Miss Carr.

"What do you think they meant, with all that chat about collectors, and publicity leaflets and all?" Dessy wondered.

"It looks as if they are planning to sell the diary, all right," said Brendan, "and to some very rich people."

"What kind of people would buy it?" asked Dessy.

"You hear about these collectors," said Molly, "the ones who buy famous stolen paintings, and keep them secretly for themselves. Perhaps it's the same kind of operation."

"Whatever it is, we've got to stop it," said Brendan. "Car-Wash said she was going to hide the diary back in the cupboard. We must get it somehow!"

"Before that," said Molly, "why don't we go to see

Miss Bright? She could call the experts who looked at the document and find out all about it."

"Maybe Locky would take us over in the morning," said Brendan.

They rang Locky at Horseshoe House.

"I was just going to ring *you*," he said. "There was another jumbled-up bunch of letters on the computer screen when we switched it on just now."

"Great, Grandpa!" said Brendan. "I'll just get my notebook out."

He took down the new message:

CZMFDQ – NUDQ RDZ

"Thanks," said Brendan, "I'll work it out right away. We just wondered, Grandpa, if you could give us a lift over to see Miss Bright the librarian tomorrow. There's something urgent we need to ask her."

"Sure," said Locky. "I'll call for you at nine o'clock. OK?"

"Great," said Brendan. "See you tomorrow."

They decoded the message. Brendan looked puzzled.

"It translates as DANGER – OVER SEA," he said.

"Maybe it means someone from abroad is the danger," said Molly.

"Could be," said Brendan. "After all, Dervla Gallagher used to live in California."

"And she's dangerous all right," said Dessy.

Joan Bright's mother lived about twenty kilometres

63

away, on the outskirts of the nearest town. She had a small house with a garden. Joan Bright opened the door to them, saying her mother was upstairs in her bedroom. She brought them into the living-room downstairs.

"I'm delighted to see you," she said. "But what you said on the phone was worrying. Sit down, and tell me about it."

"The Ballygandon Gang has found something very puzzling," said Locky.
"We suspect that your replacement librarian is not as straight as she should be."

Molly and the others told Joan Bright what Miss Carr had said about the diary being worthless. They didn't say anything about their cellar visits – they thought Locky and Miss Bright might think they were inventing it all. They wanted to know first what the Dublin experts had to say.

"I'll ring Gemma Danaher straight away," said Joan. She went into the hall.

"Gemma Danaher!" said Locky, turning to Molly. "That's my old friend – you remember her, don't you?"

The Ballygandon Gang certainly remembered Gemma Danaher. She was the historical expert who had helped them save the ancient monument at Horseshoe House, and saved the toy horse made of silver they had found in the circus field.

Locky went to have a word with his friend on the

phone, and they heard him say: "Well, Gemma, we'll find out what's happened to the diary. The Ballygandon Gang is on the trail." He came back into the room with Joan Bright.

"What did she say?" asked Molly.

"The diary is real," said Locky. "Gemma says she sent it back to the library, with translations and certificates and everything."

8

A Stolen Disguise

"Then where can the diary be?" said Joan Bright. "This is very alarming. I was going to phone Evanna Carr about my talk at the library on Thursday – I'll ask her about the diary."

She went into the hall to the telephone.

Brendan whispered to Molly: "Do you think we should tell her?"

"I don't think so," Molly whispered back. "We don't want to let Miss Carr know that we've found out her secret. She'd take the diary away somewhere else, and we might never find it."

"What are you whispering about?" Locky asked.

"We can't tell you, Grandpa, not just yet," said Molly.

"Suit yourself," said Locky, "but in that case I won't tell you *my* secret – the horse that's going to win the 3.30 race at Fairyhouse tomorrow!"

When Joan Bright came back, her face was angry

and frowning. "That woman has got a nerve!" she said.

"What's wrong?" asked Locky.

"She told me the diary and the papers never arrived. If that's true it's really worrying. And on top of that, she said she was planning to cancel my talk at the library!"

"Why?" asked Brendan.

"So as not to take me away from looking after my mother – that's what *she* says."

"We can't stand for that," said Locky.

"I didn't," said Joan Bright. "I told her I was going ahead with it anyway."

"Well, we'll all be there, for sure," said Molly. She was thinking that during the talk they might have a chance to explore the basement again.

Just as they got home, the telephone rang. Molly's mother answered it, and turned to Molly. "It's for you," she said. "It's your friend Billy Bantam, calling from California."

Molly took the phone excitedly. Billy was the child film star they had met when he was acting in a horror movie made in Ballygandon, and later they had all been over to visit him in California.

"Hi there, Molly!" Billy said.

"Hello Billy, how are you doing?" Molly asked.

"Just fine, and I've got some great news too. I have to come to Ireland to make another movie. It's in West Cork this time."

"Hey, that's great!" said Molly. "When will you be coming?"

"At the end of the week," said Billy. "The filming doesn't start till the following week, but my mother suggested we both come over early, so we can come see you in Ballygandon."

"That's wonderful."

"By the way," said Billy, "my mother was talking to one of the big movie producers here, and he said he'd got some information about the sale of some ancient documents from an Irish castle. It couldn't be your castle in Ballygandon, could it?"

Molly's heart was beating very fast. "I don't know," she said. "Do you have any idea who's organising it?"

"Let me think – the guy did say some name to my mother . . . Yes, I remember now. It was someone called Professor Carr."

"Billy, this could be very important!" said Molly.

"How come?"

Molly told him all about Miss Carr in the library, and the discovery of Princess Ethna's diary, and how it had gone missing, and the Ballygandon Gang was on the trail.

"This is too good to miss!" Billy was excited. "I'm going to tell my mom we must catch the next plane over!"

Molly, Brendan and Dessy decided to cycle over to the town and surprise Billy and his mother by greeting them when they arrived at the big hotel there. As they rode along, Brendan said: "We've got plenty of time. Why don't we take a short detour and call at Killbreen on the way?"

"What's in Killbreen?" asked Dessy.

"That's where Seamus Gallagher's pub is. Dervla Gallagher's father. Remember she said she was hiding out there."

"What do you want to do, arrest her?" asked Molly.

"No," said Brendan. "I thought if we could see her, then I could take a secret picture of her with my camera. That would be definite proof, when we decide to call in the guards."

"Let's hit the trail then, pardners," said Dessy in his wild-west cowboy voice. He slapped the seat of his bike and cried: "Giddy-up, Silver!"

Gallagher's was a seedy-looking pub on the edge of Killbreen. The paint on the walls was peeling and the lettering of the name was faded. They stopped a hundred yards or so up the road.

"What do we do now?" asked Dessy. "We can't just march in and start taking pictures."

"We'll go round the back," said Brendan. The pub was at the end of a row of shops and houses in Killbreen's only street. There was a patch of waste ground beside it, and they wheeled their bikes across this and behind some bushes not far from the back of the building. From here they could see the back windows.

They left their bikes behind the bushes and crept forward, crouching, till they were below the windows. One window was open, and they could hear voices inside. One was Dervla's, the other belonged to her father, Seamus. They were arguing.

"I want some money up front," said Seamus. "Once you're away in America collecting the loot, how do I know I'll ever see any of it?"

"I told you I'd give you a cut, Dad. Don't you believe me?"

"I wouldn't have believed you'd have run off like that and left me to face that whole court business the last time. But you did!"

"Well, I came back, didn't I?" Dervla snapped. "At great risk, by the way. If it wasn't for that wig I've been wearing, I'd probably have been arrested by now."

"You didn't come back just to see your dear old dad, that's for sure," Seamus grumbled. "I could rot in jail for all you care."

"Oh, shut up whingeing," said Dervla. "I told you, you'll get your money."

"Before you head off to America?"

"Yes, yes, yes!" Dervla shouted.

As the argument continued, Brendan pressed himself against the wall, and very slowly began to stand up. He was just underneath the open window. As he peered over the ledge, he found he was looking into the kitchen at the back of the pub. Seamus was sitting at the table with a glass and a bottle of whiskey in front of him. Dervla was striding about the room. She had taken off her black wig.

Cautiously Brendan took the camera from his pocket and pointed it over the ledge. He focussed close-up on Dervla, and clicked. He ducked down as he saw her swivel round, wondering what the sound was.

The three of them crouched on the ground, their backs flattened against the wall. They heard Dervla's voice just above them. "Did you hear something?" she asked.

"No," said Seamus, "you're getting paranoid, imagining people following you."

"You can't be too careful," said Dervla. She peered out of the window and said: "I can't see anyone lurking about, anyway." The three figures below her held their breath. Luckily, she didn't look down. She turned and went back into the room to continue her argument with her father.

"Did you get the picture?" Molly whispered.

"I did," said Brendan, "and I saw something else as well."

"What was that?" asked Dessy.

"This!" said Brendan dramatically. He reached his hand up towards the window-sill and snatched something.

"What is it?" Molly asked, as he brought his hand down. Brendan held his hand out. In it was a straggling glossy black mass of hair. It was Dervla's wig!

"It was on the window-sill," said Brendan. "I couldn't resist it."

They heard Dervla say: "I'm sure there's someone out there." She must be coming towards the window again.

"Run for it!" cried Molly, and still crouching they scurried along the wall and dived behind the bushes. Peering through the branches, they could see the furious face of Dervla looking out of the window. Then she gave a shriek of rage.

"It's gone!" she shouted. "Someone's taken it!" Clearly Seamus must have asked a question inside the room, for she shrieked: "The wig! My black wig! It's gone! I'm going out there."

"You can't, you'll be seen!" they heard Seamus cry.

"Then *you* go! Quick, get on with it!"

"We're out of here!" said Molly. "On your bikes!" Frantically they grabbed their bikes and pedalled up the road away from the pub.

They stopped when they got back to the junction with the main road and leaned their bikes against the signpost. They sat on the patch of grass underneath it, to get their breath back.

"What a trophy, eh?" said Brendan, holding up the black wig.

"Fantastic," said Molly. "Now Dervla won't be able to go out until she finds some other disguise. That should buy us a bit of time while we get the diary back."

Dessy took the wig from Brendan and put it on. "Well, gals, how do I look?" he said, standing up and doing a wiggling walk up and down.

"Like the Wicked Witch of the West!" said Brendan.

"I'll wear this when we meet Billy," said Dessy. "I bet he won't know me."

"He won't *want* to know you," said Molly. "Hey, we'd better get going, or they'll arrive at the hotel before we do."

They leaned their bikes against the wall near the open gates of the drive that led to the front door of the hotel. They sat on the low wall and looked up the road. Billy and his mother were going to pick up their hired car at Dublin airport and drive straight down.

"Maybe this is them," said Dessy, getting ready to put on the wig. He pointed at a saloon car coming down the road.

"Oh, that's not nearly posh enough," said Molly. "There'll be a limousine for the Bantams!" And sure enough, they soon saw a long dark blue limousine making its way towards them. It slowed down to turn in at the gate.

They all began to wave. Dessy put on the wig. "Hi, Billy!" they cried. "Welcome to Ireland!" The driver in his peaked cap looked as if he would like to ignore them, but a window of the car was lowered, and Billy's head came out.

"Well, if it ain't the Ballygandon Gang!" Billy cried. He told the driver to stop, and leaped out of the car. They greeted each other with high-five salutes, and Billy said: "Hey, Dessy, you've grown your hair since we last met. It suits you!"

"Do you reckon I could get a part in the movies?" Dessy asked.

"No problem, Dessy," said Billy Bantam. "You'd make a terrific spaniel!"

Billy's mother was delighted to see them again, and insisted they all had coffee and soft drinks in the hotel lounge. Soon she said she was tired after the journey and would like to go up to the room and rest.

They were able to tell Billy all about the diary and what they had discovered. They all agreed it was best not to tell Billy's mother – just as they had not told Joan Bright or Locky the full story yet. They were afraid they would immediately call in the Guards and alert Miss Carr and Dervla, who might even destroy the diary to get rid of the evidence.

They agreed to meet Billy and his mother at the library the next evening, when Joan Bright was giving her talk.

In the library, the central bookstacks had been wheeled back to give room for rows of chairs. There was a platform at one end of the big room, with chairs and a table.

Brendan, Molly and Dessy hung round the entrance to the library, waiting for Billy and his mother.

Miss Carr arrived, and said sarcastically: "You three had better go inside to make sure you get seats. I am sure there will be a *huge* audience for Miss Bright's little talk."

Just then they saw the limousine draw up. Miss Carr watched curiously, as Billy Bantam and his mother got out. Mrs Bantam was wearing a purple dress and a scarlet cloak. She had a hat with a long red feather waving from it, and was made up as if she was about to go on the stage. Billy followed her out of the car, wearing a smart grey suit and a bow tie.

Miss Carr gazed at them in astonishment. Molly stepped forward. "Oh, Miss Carr, I'd like you to meet our friends, Mrs Bantam from Hollywood, and her son Billy, the famous film star."

"How do you do?" said Billy's mother graciously, holding out her hand. Miss Carr shook it, her eyes wide. Then she shook hands with Billy too.

"I'm sure this is going to be a great show!" said Billy's mother, and with a stately walk, she went into the library.

9

Treasures

There were about forty people gathered in the library for the talk. They looked up in amazement as Mrs Bantam made her entrance, crying: "Good evening, fans!"

Molly's parents got up and came across to greet her and Billy, whom they had got to know during the filming of the horror movie.

"Are we going to have some movies tonight?" Billy asked, pointing at the screen that was set up at the back of the platform.

"No, just slides," said Joan Bright. "My talk is about the treasures of Ballygandon, and I've got pictures of some of the objects from the Ballygandon Hoard that was found here a few years ago. They're all in the National Museum now."

"Well, that's truly wonderful," said Billy's mother. "I just love that Old World stuff."

Miss Carr came across to them and said: "Well, I

think it's time we started, don't you? The sooner we begin, the sooner we can all get away."

She clearly meant this to be a sneer at Miss Bright, but the librarian ignored it, and went across to the platform. She smiled at the audience, and said: "Well now, if everyone's settled, I'll begin."

Billy Bantam started clapping. Everyone was a bit surprised, but soon they all joined in. Joan Bright looked startled. When the applause had finished she smiled again and said: "Thank you. Thank you very much. Now, as you know, my talk tonight is about the treasures of Ballygandon . . ."

Brendan, Molly and Dessy were at the back. They listened until Joan Bright said: "Now, if we could have the lights dimmed, I can show you some slides of the Ballygandon Hoard. Miss Carr, perhaps you would oblige." She pointed at the light switches beside the door.

Miss Carr didn't look too pleased, but she went across and flicked a few switches.

There was now just one light on, near the entrance. Joan Bright picked up the remote-control button for changing the slides, and clicked it. A picture came on to the screen, showing a bronze bowl decorated with jewels.

"This is known as the High King's bowl," said Miss Bright. "It was kept for feasts on special royal occasions . . ."

In the back row, Brendan whispered to Molly:

"Now's our chance." They had drawn lots for which two of them would sneak out and go down to the basement. Dessy had lost. Brendan and Molly crept out of the row of seats and disappeared behind the bookstacks at the back of the room. They went to the door of the basement and opened it slowly. When they were inside, at the top of the stairs, Molly closed the door carefully.

They didn't like to switch on the light in case it showed under the door in the darkness of the library. The basement was pitch dark. Molly gripped the top of the stair-rail. Brendan got his torch out of his pocket and switched it on. The beam picked out the stairs below them. Slowly they made their way down.

It felt damp and cold in the basement, and Molly could easily believe there were unseen presences lurking in the shadows. She shivered. She mustn't let herself start imagining things. Brendan asked her to hold the torch. He picked up the piece of wood they had used to probe the hiding-place of the tube with the rolled-up diary in it, at the back of the cupboard.

"I took a lesson from Car-Wash this time," said Brendan softly. "I brought a magnet." He rummaged in his pocket and brought out a large horse-shoe-shaped magnet and a piece of string. "Shine the torch for me, Molly, and I'll tie the magnet to the end of the stick."

He was kneeling down in front of the cupboard, tying on the magnet, when Molly said: "Oh no! I don't believe it!"

"What's up?" asked Brendan.

"Look at the cupboard."

Brendan looked up, as Molly shone the torch on the cupboard doors. They were fastened together with a large padlock.

"Damn!" said Brendan. "That's Car-Wash's doing, I suppose. An extra precaution."

"We could do with some help from Dessy's brother after all," said Molly with a smile. "I'm sure that picking locks is among his talents."

"At least it shows the documents are still in there, otherwise she wouldn't bother to lock them in," said Brendan. "But we're going to need more than a magnet to sort out that lock."

"Hey, I've just thought of something," said Molly, worried. "What's happened to Internet?"

"She couldn't have locked her in there, surely?" Brendan wondered.

"I wouldn't put it past her."

They began to call in low tones: "Internet! Internet! Puss, puss, puss!" Brendan flashed the torch all around the basement. There was no sign of the cat. Then they heard a *miaow* in the darkness. It came from the direction of the cupboard. Brendan swung the torch-beam around.

From the narrow gap between the back of the cupboard and the wall appeared a black furry head. It was Internet! The cat blinked in the light, then squeezed with some effort out of the gap and came towards them, purring.

"Thank goodness you're safe, Internet," said Molly. "Here you are." She took a paper bag out of her pocket and sprinkled some dry cat-food on the ground. Internet began munching it eagerly.

"I wish I had an elastic body like you, Internet," Molly grinned. "I could get into that cupboard with no bother."

"We'll have to leave it for now, I'm afraid," said Brendan, pulling at the lock. "We'd better get back to the library."

Leaving the cat to finish her meal, they went up the stairs. Soon they were back in their seats.

"What's the scene?" Dessy whispered. They told him about the locked cupboard. "That's tough," Dessy said.

"Now," said Joan Bright from the platform, "we come to what we might call the star attraction, though it is rather a tragic one."

She clicked her remote-control switch. On to the screen came a picture of an elaborate Celtic brooch with a long pin attached to the back to fasten it.

Miss Bright went on: "This beautiful brooch belonged to Princess Ethna, who came to Ballygandon Castle to marry the chieftain's son Fergal. There was a great feast on the night before the wedding. Suddenly they noticed that Princess Ethna was missing. People went to search for her, and she was found lying in the tower – the one that is still standing among the ruins on the hill. She was dead. Stabbed in the heart with the pin of that very brooch."

"Wow!" Billy Bantam exclaimed.

"What a truly tragic story," said his mother. "Truly tragic!"

"It was indeed," said Joan Bright, "and the murder began a feud between the two clans which lasted for centuries."

"Say," said Billy, "doesn't the Princess's ghost still haunt the castle?"

"Some people claim she does," said Miss Bright, "and there have even been rumours that her presence is felt in other places too. I had been hoping to show you a further rare treasure that has been discovered, down in the basement of this very library, which used to be a gate-lodge at the entrance to the castle grounds. It appears to be a diary that was kept by Princess Ethna herself . . ."

Just then there was a thud at the back of the library, as if something had crashed to the floor. Everyone looked round. "What was that?" asked Mrs Bantam.

Molly got up and went behind the bookstack. She came back carrying a large book. She held it up so that Miss Bright could see it, and said: "It was this book, Miss Bright. It fell off the shelf. It's a book of ghost stories."

There was another thud, then another. They all looked at the bookstack. It seemed to be rocking about, as if someone was pushing it. More books fell out of it. Then the stack rocked violently and fell backwards, crashing to the ground and scattering books all over the floor.

"What's happening?" shrieked Mrs Bantam. Everyone else was talking and shouting too. It was almost as if some kind of earthquake had shaken the room. Then all of a sudden the single light beside the door started flickering on and off. A strange sighing sound filled the air, like a whistling wind.

"It's Princess Ethna, come to haunt us!" cried Billy.

"Don't be ridiculous!" snapped Miss Carr.

"A ghost?" said Mrs Bantam. "I can handle ghosts! It's all in Shakespeare!"

"What is she on about?" asked Locky.

Mrs Bantam struck a theatrical pose, her right arm held high. Then she began to speak in a ringing voice:

"Angels and ministers of grace defend us!
Be thou a spirit of health or goblin damn'd,
Bring with thee airs from heaven or blasts from hell,
Be thy intents wicked or charitable,
Thou com'st in such a questionable shape
That I will speak to thee!"

Everyone was so amazed at this performance that they almost forgot the weird things that had happened. They all stood where they were, gazing at Mrs Bantam in astonishment. Then Dessy shouted "Bravo!" and began to clap. Billy joined in, so did Molly and Dessy. Everyone else just looked on, bewildered. Mrs Bantam bowed graciously to the audience.

The light had stopped flickering, and the strange sighing sound could be heard no longer. There was an eerie silence in the room.

"You see – it worked!" said Mrs Bantam. "Just as well I learnt *Hamlet* during my theatre training."

"Nonsense," said Miss Carr, "there are no ghosts here."

"And no diary either?" asked Molly.

"Of course not," said Miss Carr. "I explained all about the diary to Miss Bright. It's gone astray. I'm sure it will turn up eventually. Now if some of you will help me, I'd like to get this mess cleared up and the books back in place."

Molly's father, with Locky and the Ballygandon Gang, managed to raise the big bookstack back into place. Then they began picking up the scattered books and putting them back on the shelves, with Miss Carr instructing them.

"Perhaps the diary got put into one of these shelves by mistake," said Billy innocently, examining one of the books.

"Yes, or it might be lost somewhere else in the library," said Molly.

"Perhaps we should make a search," said Dessy. "Upstairs and downstairs."

When he said "downstairs" Miss Carr glanced at him with a beady-eyed frown. Molly thought she must be wondering if they knew more than they pretended.

"I tell you they are not here!" said Miss Carr sharply. "Now let's get on with these shelves."

Billy said casually as they went on working, "Say, Miss Carr, have you got family over in the States?"

"A distant cousin in Chicago, that's all," Miss Carr replied.

"I was thinking of California, where we come from," said Billy. Molly looked at him in alarm. She was afraid he would give away what they knew. She stared at Billy and gave a shake of her head.

But Billy just winked at her, and went on: "It's just that a friend of my mother's heard of some documents from an Irish castle that are being sold over in Los Angeles, and it's all being arranged by someone called Professor Carr. I just wondered if it was any relation?"

Brendan and Molly looked at each other anxiously. Surely Billy had gone too far.

"The eejit!" Brendan whispered. "He'll ruin everything." Miss Carr was looking pale. "No relation!" she said sharply. "I don't know what you're talking about."

"There are bound to be lots of Carrs in America," said Brendan quickly.

"And lots of car-washes!" said Dessy jokily.

"We can leave the rest of the books till tomorrow," said the librarian. She turned to the people in the room, who were chatting together about the strange events of the evening.

"All's well that ends well," said Miss Carr briskly. "Time to end the performance for now. Thank you, Miss Bright, for your most interesting talk." She smiled sarcastically at Miss Bright, but before she could go on, Billy's mother interrupted.

"As a visitor to your town," she said, "may I also

thank you most sincerely, Miss Bright, for such a lively and entertaining, and indeed sometimes alarming evening! We rarely encounter the spirit world in our country, but in your ancient land, the past and the present naturally mingle in sometimes strange ways . . ."

"Thank you very much for those comments," said Miss Carr hastily, trying to shut Mrs Bantam up. But Billy's mother went on:

"What a pity that the celebrated diary of Princess Ethna was not available for us to see, but perhaps one day . . ."

"What with Billy *and* his mother going on about it," whispered Brendan to Molly, "Car-Wash will soon tumble to the fact that we're on her trail."

"Maybe we should say we know where it is," whispered Molly.

"But we *don't* know for sure," said Brendan, "and if Car-Wash thinks we do, she'll have it rushed away before we can do anything."

Suddenly Locky called out: "Hey! Look! On the screen!"

A new picture was showing on the slide screen.

Miss Carr said: "Miss Bright, I thought I said we would call a halt to the evening."

"But I was just packing up the slides," said Joan Bright.

"Then what's that?" asked Mrs Bantam. "It looks like some kind of old-time writing. I can't read a word of it."

"I think it's Old Irish," said Molly. "Like Princess Ethna would have written."

"It must be part of her diary!" Brendan exclaimed.

The words on the screen began to flash on and off.

"That's enough of your games, Miss Bright," said Miss Carr. "Turn off that slide projector!"

"But it isn't on!" said Joan Bright. "And besides, I haven't *got* any slides of the diary!"

10

The Haunted Tower

The strange words on the screen were still flashing on and off. People stood gaping at the screen in bewilderment. The sighing sound they had heard before seemed to fill the room again.

Miss Carr shrieked: "This is some trick! Take down that screen!" She rushed towards the platform and stepped on to it, pushing Joan Bright aside. The words were still flashing. Miss Carr was in front of the screen, so that the words seemed to be written across her face as well as on the screen. She grabbed the top of the screen and pulled. The screen and its stand came toppling towards her. She stumbled and fell, and the screen came down on top of her.

The sighing sound stopped and the glowing words had disappeared. Once again there was silence. It was broken by the spluttering and cursing of Miss Carr, as she crawled out from underneath the screen.

"Imagine Car-Wash knowing words like that!" whispered Dessy.

They all stared at Miss Carr as she stood up, her hair straggling, and patted herself down, trying desperately to keep some dignity. "The show is over!" she snapped. "Everyone please leave. The library is closing!"

The audience, who had not expected such an unusual and riotous entertainment, filed slowly through the door, talking excitedly.

"What time will you open tomorrow, Miss Carr?" asked Molly casually as she went through the door.

"We shall *not* open tomorrow. In fact we shall not open at all until everything is sorted out."

"But you can't do that," said Joan Bright.

"I can and I will," said Miss Carr. "Don't forget, I am in charge here now, not you!" She shooed the remainder of the group out, and followed them. She slammed the door behind her and locked it. Then she strode away down the road.

Next day the Ballygandon Gang went to the library. There was a notice on the door in big letters: LIBRARY CLOSED UNTIL FURTHER NOTICE.

"Now there's no way we can get into the basement," said Molly.

"We must have a Council of War," said Brendan. "Let's go up to the castle."

They sat in the courtyard of the castle, with their backs against the ruined outer wall.

"Well, that was some evening!" said Billy Bantam.

"It was!" said Brendan angrily. "And you may have wrecked everything!"

"What do you mean?" said Billy, "I was only having a bit of fun with that Car-Wash woman."

"Yes, and now she probably realises we know where the diary is hidden!" said Brendan.

"That's right," said Molly, "and she's closed the library and is maybe getting ready to move it somewhere else."

"Hey, you guys, I'm sorry," said Billy. "I thought it might get her rattled."

"I'd say it's done that all right," said Brendan. "I bet she and Dervla are plotting right now to get the diary away to America."

"Dervla won't risk going out, not until she gets a new one of these!" said Molly, putting her hand into the tote-bag she was carrying, and producing the black wig.

Billy laughed. "That's great," he said, "put it on."

Molly did so, and struck a glamorous pose. "How do I look?" she asked.

"Terrific!" said Billy, "we'll have you in the movies yet."

"Stop trick-acting, you two!" said Brendan gruffly. "This is serious. Car-Wash may be already moving the diary from the basement."

"No, she's not," said Dessy.

"How do you know?" Brendan asked.

"Look," Dessy said. He pointed out through a big gap in the wall where the stones had fallen away.

They peered through. "See, down at the bottom of the hill," said Dessy.

There, where the road ended and a gate led to the path up the hill, a white van was parked. Miss Carr was pacing up and down beside it. Every now and then she looked at her watch, then looked down the road towards the town.

"She must be waiting for someone," said Billy.

"Probably Dervla," said Molly.

"Well, she's not waiting for the Guards, that's for sure!" said Dessy. "Hey, what did the explorer say when he saw what was in the Egyptian tomb?"

"What, Dessy?" said Brendan impatiently.

"Hello, Mummy!" said Dessy, delighted with himself.

Before they could even groan at Dessy, Brendan cried: "Car-Wash is looking this way. Duck!" They all ducked down, but Molly wasn't quite in time. Miss Carr had seen her head with the black wig on, peeping through the gap.

"Dervla!" she shouted. "You're late. What on earth are you doing up there?"

"The wig!" said Molly, as they huddled out of sight by the wall. "She saw me, and thought it was Dervla. She must have arranged to meet her there."

They heard Miss Carr calling angrily: "Dervla! Dervla! Come down here this minute!"

"What shall we do?" asked Billy.

"Just lie low till she gets fed up and goes away," said Brendan.

"Too late for that," said Dessy, peering through a slit in the stones. "She's coming up the hill." They took it in turns to look. Indeed, Miss Carr was climbing the path towards the castle.

Halfway up she stopped and called out: "Dervla, I saw you there! This is no time for games. Come down here!" She stared up at the castle. They all held their breath and looked at each other.

"We'll have to make a run for it," said Dessy.

"She'd see us," said Brendan, "and you've seen what she's like when she's in a rage. Who knows what she might do when she realises we've been fooling around pretending to be Dervla?" He looked at Molly with a frown.

"How was I to know she'd see me in the wig?" said Molly.

"You should have ducked earlier," said Brendan.

"Listen, folks," said Billy. "Sort out your fights later. Car-Wash is on the war-path again." He was peering through the slit in the wall. "Take a look."

He stood aside and Molly looked through. She saw Miss Carr stop and call out: "Dervla! Have you gone crazy? This isn't a game of hide-and-seek. We've got no time to lose." She waited, then went on: "OK, I'll come up there."

She went on climbing the path towards them.

"She'll be in the courtyard in a minute," said Brendan. "We'll have to hide."

"Where?" asked Dessy, looking around at the ruins and the tumbled stones.

Suddenly Molly said: "Over there! In Princess Ethna's tower. She won't go into that."

"She's not the only one," said Billy. "That tower is dangerous. The staircase is crumbling away."

"We only need to go up part of the way. It's a spiral staircase. Once we're round a corner, she won't see us from down below, even if she looks into the tower."

"You're right, Molly," said Dessy. "That plan is the only game in town."

They heard Miss Carr calling: "Dervla! Wait there!"

"OK, let's go!" said Brendan. They all ran and scrambled across the stony courtyard to the tall half-ruined tower on the far side. At the entrance, they stopped for a moment.

"Are you sure this is a good idea?" asked Billy.

"Don't worry, Billy," said Dessy. "The ghosts won't get you!"

"I'm not frightened," said Billy unconvincingly.

"Nor am I," said Dessy.

"Then you go first," Billy smiled.

"Right!" said Dessy boldly. "Here I go!" He went into the entrance of the tower and began to climb the stone stairs inside. Brendan followed, then Molly. Billy hovered outside the doorway.

"Come on, Billy!" Molly turned back and stretched out her hand. "Here, hold on to me!"

This was too much for Billy Bantam. "Do you think I'm scared?" he cried, and ran through the entrance, nearly knocking Molly down as he scrambled up the stairs.

Miss Carr was in the courtyard now, gazing around. They heard her calling: "Dervla! Where are you? Stop this nonsense!"

"Go on, go up further!" hissed Molly. "She mustn't see us."

There wasn't room for them to pass each other, so Dessy had to lead the way. He began to wish he hadn't given such a show of bravery and dashed into the tower first. But there was nothing to be done about it now. "OK, forward march!" he said.

Step by step, he slowly climbed the dusty stone stairway, gripping the central column with one hand and steadying himself with his other hand on the opposite wall. The others followed. Light filtered down from the open roof of the tower and through the vertical slits in the wall where the archers would have fired their arrows at invaders below. Now the only 'invader' was a thieving librarian with no respect for the history of this place. Yet to the Ballygandon Gang just now she seemed as much of a threat as any troop of armed soldiers.

Suddenly Dessy stopped and pushed his back against the wall to steady himself. He looked back at the others and held up his hand. "Hold it!" he said.

"What's up?" asked Brendan.

"There's no more stairs," said Dessy. "Just empty air."

"That's right, I remember now," said Molly. "The top part of the stairway has fallen down."

"We can't go any further," said Dessy, "and we sure can't jump down. We're twenty metres above the ground."

"What can we do?" asked Billy, his voice shaky. He never liked heights, and now here he was looking back down a curving staircase way above the ground, with nothing to hold on to. He felt dizzy. He sat down on a step.

"You're right, Billy," said Molly kindly. "All we can do is sit here and wait."

She sat down too, but as she did so she suddenly realised that she had been standing beside one of the arrow-slits in the wall, and that part of it had fallen away, so that the gap was quite large. She hoped Car-Wash hadn't seen her head inside the tower. But her luck was out.

"There you are, Dervla!" came the rasping voice from below. "What on earth do you think you're doing up there?"

"She must have seen me," said Molly, "through that gap in the wall."

"At least she doesn't know it's you," said Dessy. "That wig fooled her."

"It's not going to be much use if she comes any closer," said Billy. "We're trapped, and that's a fact."

"Maybe she won't come any closer," said Dessy hopefully.

But then they heard Miss Carr's voice at the bottom of the stairway. "Listen to me, Dervla Gallagher!" she called. "I've had enough of this tomfoolery – and if you're not going to help, I shall just go it alone and you'll get nothing. Do you hear me – *nothing!* I can organise the American end of the sale without your local know-how, and believe me, I will. The problem is, those horrible kids from Ballygandon and that *odious* American boy suspect that I have something to do with the disappearance of that diary."

Sitting on the gloomy stairway, the Ballygandon Gang raised their fists in triumph. Dessy held his nose and pointed at Billy, mouthing the word odious. Billy grinned and made a horror face, rolling his eyes.

"Now listen carefully, Dervla," said Miss Carr. "Before those kids find out where the diary is, we've got to get it out of the library basement and find a new hiding-place, so we're ready to take it to the airport. And we've got to get it out tonight!"

There was a pause.

"I wish we had a tape-recorder," said Molly. "We'd have enough evidence to get Car-Wash locked up."

"I've got my camera," said Brendan.

"Good," said Molly, "that could come in useful."

"Her face would *break* the camera!" said Dessy, grinning.

Then they heard Miss Carr at the bottom of the stairway, shouting: "All right, Dervla, that's it! If you won't come down, I'll come up to you. I don't know what you think you're at, hiding in a haunted tower, but we've got to sort this thing out."

They heard the sound of Miss Carr's feet on the stairs, coming up slowly, one by one.

"She thinks the tower's haunted," said Molly.

"So do I," said Dessy. "I can practically hear Princess Ethna creeping about."

Miss Carr's footsteps were coming nearer up the stairs.

Molly said: "Then let's give Miss Carr a haunting, shall we?" She took out her tin whistle and began to play a sad, eerie melody.

11

Trapped!

The footsteps stopped.

There were a few moments of silence, then Miss Carr called, in an uncertain voice: "Dervla? Is that you, Dervla?"

Molly stopped playing. They heard Miss Carr say to herself: "The wind, I suppose…" They heard her footsteps start again on the stairs. Molly started playing again, but this time Miss Carr came on up the stairway. Before long she would see them crouched at the top.

Molly whispered: "There's only one thing we can do."

"What's that?" asked Brendan.

"Scare her away. She thinks I'm Dervla, right? So let her think that Dervla is being attacked, by the ghost of Princess Ethna. That should frighten her off."

They heard Miss Carr, very near now, call again: "Dervla? Dervla?" Her voice sounded shaky.

"How will you make her think Dervla's being attacked?" whispered Dessy.

"Like this," said Molly. To the surprise of them all, she gave a loud, piercing scream, then another.

Below, Miss Carr stopped and cried out in alarm: "Dervla, is that you? What's happening?"

Molly cried in a strangled voice: "The ghost! The ghost of Princess Ethna! I'm being strangled!" She screamed again.

Miss Carr said: "A ghost? It can't be . . ."

Molly shrieked: "Keep away, Evanna! You're cursed! Run now, or it will kill me! Please run for it!"

"But Dervla . . ." Miss Carr's voice was trembling.

"Go! Now!" said Molly. Brendan had an idea. He picked up a loose stone about as big as his fist, and held it up. Molly nodded. He pitched it forward on to the stairs and they heard it tumble and bump on the steps. Miss Carr gave a cry of fear.

"Go! Go!" cried Molly. As she screamed again, Dessy picked up another stone and threw it on the stairs. Then Billy did the same.

Now they heard Miss Carr scream. They tumbled more stones down the stairs and they heard her give a cry of pain and shout: "My leg!" As the clatter went on, they heard her footsteps running down the stairs. "I'm going, I'm going!" she cried.

Dessy peered through an arrow-slit in the wall. "She's running off across the courtyard. She's got to the outer wall. Now she's looking back."

Molly gave a final, piercing scream.

"That's done it!" said Dessy. "She's scrambled

through a gap in the wall and run off down the hill."

"Wow!" said Billy. "Congratulations, you guys!"

"Congratulations to us all," said Brendan. They stood up and gave high-five signs to each other. Dessy was so enthusiastic he wobbled on the top step and almost toppled down.

"Let's get out of here before we do ourselves some damage," he said. "Molly was so good, I almost thought she *was* being strangled!"

There was a faint, chuckling laugh that echoed round the tower.

"You even laugh like a ghost!" Dessy grinned.

"That wasn't me," said Molly. They all looked at each other.

"Then who . . . ?" Brendan wondered.

They heard the faint laugh again.

"Let's go!" said Billy. The others needed no more encouragement. They all clattered down the stairs after him, as fast as they could go. They ran across the courtyard till they reached the outer wall, then stopped to get their breath back. Brendan looked through a gap.

"There goes Car-Wash's van, away down the road," he said.

They sat with their backs against the wall and gazed across the courtyard at the tower, thinking of the Princess who had written that hopeful diary, only to be murdered there just before her wedding.

"We have to get that diary back, for Ethna's sake," said Molly.

"But how?" asked Dessy. "The library's shut up, and the cupboard's padlocked. Maybe we *should* get my brother down here, after all."

"Not a good idea, Dessy," said Brendan hastily. He thought that if Dessy's brother knew the diary was valuable, he might well run off with it himself.

"Anyway," said Molly, "there isn't time. Car-Wash plans to move that diary tonight. You heard her."

"I think it's time we told the Guards," said Billy.

"But would they believe us?" Dessy wondered.

"At least they'd have to search, wouldn't they?"

Brendan said: "They'd have to ask Car-Wash, and she'd just say it was a load of kids' nonsense."

"It's worth a try," said Billy. "What else can we do?"

There was silence. None of them could think of another plan.

A few minutes went by. Molly began to play a slow tune on her tin whistle. Dessy started practising tricks with his yoyo.

Suddenly Brendan said: "Hey, listen! What was that?"

Molly stopped playing. "What?" she asked.

Brendan said: "I thought I heard . . ."

Then they all heard it: a distinct *miaow*. . . .

They looked across the courtyard in the direction of the sound. There she was – a black cat with white paws, sniffing the air and waving her tail.

"It's Internet!" cried Brendan, as they all rushed across to the cat.

Brendan picked her up and stroked her. The cat began to purr happily.

"How on earth did she get up here?" asked Billy.

"I don't know," said Molly, "but I bet she's hungry." She took some dry cat-food out of her tote-bag and put it on the ground. Brendan put down the cat, who began to munch it noisily.

"Are you sure it's the same cat?" asked Dessy. "Last time you saw her she was locked up in the basement."

"That's right," said Brendan, "we thought she'd been locked into the cupboard with the diary, but then she squeezed out through a hole at the back."

Internet finished the cat-food and licked her lips. Then she prowled across the courtyard towards the wall. She looked back, almost as if she expected them to follow her. Then she went to the part of the wall where they had found the hidden hollow. She began to scratch at the ground. Then all of a sudden she disappeared.

"Internet!" cried Molly, alarmed. "What's happened to you?" They rushed across to where they had last seen her. There was a gap between the stones which covered up the hollow. Down inside, they heard a familiar *miaow.* . . .

"Quick, get the stones away!" said Brendan, pulling at them. They got the stones to one side, and there in the hollow was Internet, quite unharmed, looking up at them.

Brendan knelt down and examined the ground. "That's it!" he said excitedly. "These are the scratches I saw before, on the stones. The cat must have made them."

"So she was here before?" asked Dessy.

"Must have been," said Brendan.

"So she made those scratches trying to get in there," said Billy.

"Or getting out!" said Brendan. "That's the answer! Remember those stories about secret passages? Internet must have found one, leading from the basement, all the way up to the castle!"

"You mean there's a passage inside that wall?" said Molly.

"That's right!" said Brendan – and as though she wanted to show he was right, Internet jumped up and poked her head through a gap in the stones of the wall. Then she disappeared inside. "You see!" said Brendan triumphantly. "She's telling us!"

"Why would they have made a passage like that?" Billy asked.

"The library was originally a gate-lodge at the entrance to the castle grounds," said Molly. "They probably wanted an escape route, in case of a siege or whatever."

"So now *we* can use it, to get into the basement and rescue the diary!" Brendan exclaimed.

"Sure," said Dessy. "All we need to do is shrink ourselves to the size of a cat, and we're in business!"

"Very funny, Dessy," said Brendan. "Stop joking and help me move some of these stones."

They wrenched and pulled at the stones in the wall and succeeded in getting some of them loose. They pulled some more and one of the big stones came away and fell to the ground, nearly crushing Dessy's foot. He gave a yelp – and so did Internet, as she leaped back through the hole, out of the passage and into the courtyard. The hole was just wide enough for Brendan to poke his head in. He took out his torch and shone it around inside.

"What did you see?" asked Molly when he emerged again, brushing dust off his head.

"There's a passage all right!" Brendan was very excited. "A kind of tunnel that runs downwards. I could only see about twenty metres into it, then it curved away into the distance."

"We've got to get in there!" said Molly. She borrowed Brendan's torch and peered into the hole herself. When she came out, she said: "If we could pull one or two more stones away, we could just about squeeze inside."

They wrenched at the other stones, and two more came away and crashed to the ground. Dessy was quick enough to jump out of the way this time. They stood and looked at the gap they had made in the wall.

"It's big enough for us to climb through now," said Brendan. He moved forward and clambered into the hole, struggling a bit to squeeze through. He turned and poked his head back out. "Nothing to it!" he said. "We're on our way to the library!"

"There's a problem," said Molly. "We got these stones out all right, but what about the other end? It looked really blocked up with big stones at the back of that cupboard. Supposing we got there and found we couldn't get through?"

"Anyone know where we could get some dynamite?" asked Dessy.

"I'm serious, Dessy," said Molly. "Even if we can get all the way down the passage, we might be blocked right at the end."

"We'll just have to risk it," said Brendan. "We haven't got time to go and get crow-bars and spades and stuff."

"Hey," said Dessy, "what about the fence down there?"

"What fence?" asked Billy.

"The one round the field at the bottom of the hill," said Dessy. "It's an electric fence, with those long metal spikes stuck into the ground with the wire going along between them. Those spikes would be OK to stick between stones and lever them apart. Come on Brendan, you've got your fancy penknife, you can cut the wire, and we'll grab two or three of the spikes and bring them back up here."

"OK, Dessy," said Brendan. "But why don't I lend *you* the knife and let *you* cut the wire? I'm sure you're not afraid of a little electric shock!"

"Well, we'll talk about that when we get there," said Dessy uncertainly. The two of them went through the gap in the wall and began to scramble down the hill towards the field below.

They stood together beside the fence. Brendan got out his penknife with all its folding blades. He fiddled with it. "This is the right gadget," he said. "It's like a miniature pair of pliers. It should be strong enough to cut that wire. Here you are, Dessy." He held out the penknife.

Dessy didn't take it. "You have a go first, Brendan," he said. "You understand those yokes better than I do."

"It's dead simple," said Brendan, "you just press it like this and the two sides click together and cut the wire. It won't do you any harm. After all, you've got rubber shoes. They'll insulate you."

"You've got rubber shoes too," Dessy pointed out.

"Yours are thicker," said Brendan.

Dessy turned and looked up towards the castle, as if seeking for some kind of help. He saw Molly and Billy peering through a gap in the wall, clearly wondering why they were hanging about down here. "Oh, all right!" he told Brendan. "Give it here!"

Dessy grabbed the penknife and snapped the wire with the pliers. He felt a sharp tingle in his arm, but nothing more. But he decided to get his own back on Brendan. He grasped the penknife with both hands and fell to the ground, writhing about and giving cries of pain.

Brendan knelt down and grabbed his shoulders. "Dessy! Dessy! Are you all right?" he shouted. Dessy went on writhing and screeching. "Don't worry, Dessy, just stay there. I'll run and get an ambulance!" Brendan was about to run off towards the road.

From up at the castle, they heard Molly shout: "What's happened?" Then they saw Molly and Billy leap through the gap in the outer wall and start running down the hill towards them. Dessy realised things were getting out of control. He sat up.

"I'm OK," he said. "A bit of a jolt, that's all." He shook his head around, like a dog drying itself after a swim. "Close thing, that," he said.

"You're a great fella, Dessy," said Brendan.

Molly and Billy came scrambling down the hill.

"Dessy, are you OK?" said Molly. "We saw you cut the wire, and then fall down."

"No problem," said Dessy, "just a bit of a shock, that's all. Let's get the metal spikes out, eh?"

"You're a brave guy, Dessy," said Billy.

"A star!" said Molly, as they began to take the metal fence-spikes out of the ground.

"Sure, it was nothing," said Dessy. All this praise was making him start to believe that he really *had* survived great danger.

As they began to climb back up the hill, each of them carrying one of the metal spikes, Dessy said: "Hey, what do you call a cream bun heated up by electricity?"

"Tell us, Dessy," said Brendan.

"A *CURRENT BUN!*" said Dessy.

They were all so relieved that Dessy was back to his normal jokey self, that instead of groaning, they all laughed loudly.

When they got back up the hill and into the castle courtyard, Internet was there to greet them. Molly picked her up. "You're a star too, Internet," she said. The cat gave a satisfied purr.

"Right!" said Brendan, waving his metal spike in the air. "The Ballygandon Gang is on the war-path. Or rather, down the passage!"

They all brandished their spikes and cheered, as they lined up to follow Brendan into the hole that led to the tunnel. As she prepared to clamber in, Molly looked back at the ruined tower on the other side of the courtyard. Was it her imagination, or did she hear once again that faint, chuckling laugh . . . ?

12

The Secret Passage

"Is everyone in?" asked Brendan, shining his torch back towards the entrance.

"Aye-aye, Captain," said Dessy.

Brendan could see the three dark figures behind him, black against the light outside the tunnel entrance. Then he saw another silhouette: Internet the cat was sitting in the opening of the tunnel. She gave a loud *miaow* and jumped down into the passage. Then she sidled past them and began to walk down the tunnel ahead of them.

"Internet is leading the way," said Molly, as Brendan followed the cat, shining his torch on it. The tunnel sloped downwards and was sometimes so low that they had to crouch down so as not to bump their heads on the roof of it. The stones that formed the walls were rough and jagged, and several times they scraped their arms as they squeezed through the narrow parts.

The floor was uneven and they often stumbled as they made their way in the darkness, with only the beam of Brendan's torch to guide them. Every now and then he stopped so as to shine the torch back and let the other three see the floor of the passage.

"I bet there's a great echo in here," said Dessy. He called out loudly: "Hull-O-O-O-O!" The O seemed to drag itself out, bouncing off the walls and finally dying away.

"Be quiet, Dessy," said Brendan. "Sound-waves can dislodge rocks."

"You're kidding," said Dessy.

"I heard that somewhere, too," said Billy.

"Better not risk it, Dessy," said Molly.

They went on in silence, broken only by the shuffle and scrape of their feet on the rough stone floor. The air smelt stale and musty. Brendan thought this was what it must be like inside the tombs of the pyramids where the mummified Pharaohs waited for the after-life, surrounded by their priceless treasures.

He stopped once more and shone his torch back so the others could see where they were going. Suddenly Billy gave a cry of shock.

"What's up?" asked Brendan.

"I thought I saw . . ." Billy began, then he shook his head as if to clear it and went on: "No, it couldn't be."

"You're winding us up," said Dessy.

"No, I'm not," said Billy. "It's just that when your torch flashed along the wall just beside Dessy, I thought I saw something sticking out of the wall."

"Let's have a look," said Brendan, and he shone the torch on the wall.

They all gasped. Sticking out from a gap between two stones was a bony hand.

It seemed to be pointing at them. They stared at it for a few moments in silence.

Then Billy said softly: "Wow!"

Brendan felt the hair prickle on his scalp. Molly blinked hard several times, thinking the thing might disappear, but it still stayed there, motionless.

"There must be a skeleton buried inside there," she said.

"Buried for centuries, I should think," said Brendan.

"It can't be a grave," said Molly. "We must be far too deep down underground by now."

"Maybe there was part of the tunnel that caved in and buried whoever it was," said Brendan.

"That must be it," said Molly. "Anyway, there's nothing we can do. We'd best go on."

As they began to move forward, Dessy reached out and shook the extended hand, saying: "Bye for now!" The skeleton hand came away from the wall and he was left holding it. He gave a shriek and dropped it quickly on to the ground.

"Eejit!" said Brendan – but his voice showed how scared he was. So were they all.

"Let's get out of here, fast!" said Billy, pushing Dessy forward ahead of him.

"Good thinking," said Dessy. As they moved on hurriedly, Dessy looked back. He could just see the white bones of the hand lying on the floor of the passage. Then the tunnel curved and he could see it no more. He realised he was shivering. He wondered if his hair had gone white with the shock. But he'd feel a fool if he asked Brendan to shine the torch on it. He shook himself and trudged on.

They went on and on for what seemed hours, but Brendan looked at his watch and found they had only been about half an hour underground. Then ahead of him he saw something reflecting the torchlight. "Stop!" he called. He realised what it was: there was water on the floor of the passage.

He told the others and then moved slowly towards it. They all crowded round. Suppose they had come to an underground river they couldn't cross? But the water didn't seem to be flowing. Then a drip of water fell with a splash from the roof. Brendan shone his torch upwards. They saw that the ceiling of the tunnel was slimy and damp.

"There must be a stream up above and the water is seeping down," said Molly.

"Let's test the depth," said Brendan. He prodded his metal fence-post at the water. It only went down about thirty centimetres, the length of a ruler.

"It's not too deep," said Billy, "but we'll have soaking wet feet if we paddle through that."

"Let's jump it!" said Molly. "If we use our fence-posts to help us, we should just about get over."

"I'll go first, men," said Dessy. "Stand back." He

walked back a few paces to get a run at it. Then he cried: "Geronimo!" and rushed forward and jumped, pushing his metal spike down into the water. He just reached the other side, wobbled a bit as if he was going to fall backwards into the water, then straightened up.

"Nothing to it, folks," he said proudly.

They all got over all right, though Billy got his left foot wet at the far edge of the water. They looked back and Brendan shone his torch. Back on the other side the light reflected from the two yellow eyes of Internet. She gave a soft *miaow*.

"We can't leave her behind," said Molly. "I'm going to jump back over, and paddle back with her."

"She must have managed to cross it before," said Brendan, "or how did she get up and down the passage between the cellar and the castle?"

They soon had the answer. They saw Internet arch her back, then crouch down. She made a dash forward and leapt into the air, across the pool of water. She landed safe and sound, and dry, just in front of them. They all clapped, delighted. Molly picked up the cat and stroked her. "You really are a star, Internet," she said.

They moved on for another ten minutes.

"I hope we *can* get out at the far end," said Billy. "I don't fancy trekking all the way back."

"Ssssh!" said Brendan, stopping suddenly. "Listen, back there in the tunnel." They all stopped. Sure enough, they could hear a rumbling sound. Then there was a loud roar and a crash like thunder. Then silence.

Brendan shone his torch back along the passage. There were clouds of dust floating in the air. Gradually they subsided and the torch-beam picked out something which made them all feel a chill of fear: a pile of boulders was blocking the tunnel.

"The roof back there has fallen in," said Molly.

"We were right under there a couple of minutes ago," Dessy said.

"We couldn't go back now if we wanted to," said Brendan. He shone his torch on the roof above them. It looked solid enough, but so had the rest of the roof behind them. "We'll have to go on as fast as we can," he said.

The little procession went on in silence. They each felt that their hearts were beating so loudly they would have to be heard by the others. Finally the torch-beam shone ahead on a tumbled pile of rock, blocking the passage.

"This has to be the end of it," said Brendan.

"Let's hope it's not another rock-fall," said Billy.

"Good man, Billy," said Dessy, "always looking on the bright side!"

"There's only one way to find out," said Brendan. "Let's go to work."

He prodded his metal spike into a gap between two of the rocks, and prised them apart. He pulled one of the rocks away, and jumped back as it fell to the ground.

They all began to use their sticks to get the rocks away. Soon there was a hole through the pile of boulders. Brendan went forward and clambered on to the front of the pile. He could just get his head and shoulders into the gap. He managed to squeeze his right hand with the torch in it, in beside his ear.

"We're there!" he called back. "I can see the back of the cupboard doors!"

"Bingo!" said Dessy. "Can you see what's in there?"

Brendan pointed the torch down. "There it is!" he said. "The same book we saw before, lying on the floor of the cupboard. Before we make the hole larger, I'm going to take a photograph as evidence."

He brought out his camera and took a flashlight picture of the leather-covered diary lying at the bottom of the cupboard. Then Molly and the others took it in turns to peer through the hole at their discovery.

"OK," said Brendan, "let's get to work and make the gap large enough to crawl through."

"We'll have no problem levering the cupboard doors open with these," said Dessy, holding up his metal spike. "We can wrench the padlock off."

Once more they started to prise the rocks apart with their spikes. Then again Brendan said: "Sssh! Listen!"

"Not more rock-falls?" asked Billy.

"No," said Brendan. "Voices."

They all kept still. Through the hole they could see a light shining through a chink in the closed cupboard doors. They heard two voices. One definitely belonged to Miss Carr – they'd know that rasping, bossy tone anywhere. The other voice was Dervla's. They were arguing.

"It's just as well I found you in the end," said Dervla. "I don't know what you were doing up in that castle, thinking you saw ghosts strangling me in a haunted tower. You'd have gone stark raving mad if I hadn't calmed you down."

"You were supposed to meet me there!" snapped Miss Carr.

"I told you, Seamus's rotten old car broke down," said Dervla.

"Well, if it wasn't you in the tower, who was it?"

"I keep telling you, it must have been those horrible kids. If I ever find them they'll get more than a haunting. I'll thump them so hard they'll be glad to join the spirit world themselves."

"She'd do it, too," Dessy whispered.

"Anyway, let's get the diary away from here," said Miss Carr. "Tomorrow it's off to Los Angeles and goodbye Ballygandon, Princess Ethna and the whole damn lot of them."

"And hello to a life of luxury!" said Dervla. "Give me the key to the padlock."

"I'll open it myself," said Miss Carr sharply. Standing back from the gap so as not to be seen, Brendan and Molly heard the rattle of the padlock. Then the cupboard doors opened wide, and they saw the faces of Car-Wash and Dervla gazing down greedily at the diary which they thought was their passport to a fortune. Instead of the lost wig, Dervla was wearing a wide-brimmed black felt hat, pulled down over her face.

"We've got to stop them," Molly whispered. "I think I might be small enough to squeeze through that gap."

"You'd be no match for that pair on your own," said Brendan. "But I know one thing we can do. Get some real proof." He took his polaroid camera and pointed it through the gap, tilting it downwards. Just as the two women knelt down and picked up the diary, he took a flashlight picture. Then he stood back in the shadows.

"What was that?" they heard Dervla cry in alarm.

"It was like a flash of lightning," said Evanna Carr.

"Lightning? Down here?" said Dervla. "You *are* going off your rocker!"

"Then what was it? It seemed to come from that hole in the wall. There's someone hiding in there."

"How can there be?" said Dervla. "That's solid rock behind the cupboard."

"I know. Only the cat can get in and out of there."

"Maybe it's bought itself a sun-ray lamp," Dervla sneered. "The main thing is to get this loot out of here." She snatched up the ancient volume.

"Give that to me!" said Miss Carr, grabbing them from her.

"What's the matter?" asked Dervla. "Don't you trust me, Evanna?"

"Not an inch," said Miss Carr.

"Good," Dervla smiled. "Then we'll make a great team! Let's go!"

They turned and went up the stairs. The door to the basement closed behind them.

"I'm going after them!" said Molly, beginning to wriggle through the gap in the wall.

"You can't risk it, Molly!" said Brendan. "You heard what she said she'd do."

But Molly was halfway through the gap. She got her hands through and pushed at the edges of the gap. She fell down on to the floor of the cupboard.

"Molly, stop!" Dessy shouted.

Molly picked herself up. "I'm going to follow them!" she said. "We've got to know where they take the diary!"

"Molly! Molly! Come back!" All three of the others were calling out now. But they saw Molly rush up the basement stairs and out of the door into the library.

13

The Final Chase

"We've got to go after her!" said Brendan, pushing frantically at the stones beside the gap. "She could be in terrible danger."

As he spoke, he felt something brush his arm. It was Internet. The cat leaped through the gap and on to the floor of the cupboard, then raced across the basement and up the stairs.

"We must get these stones away and go after Molly," said Brendan. They all pushed and wrenched at the stones. It took them a few minutes to dislodge two of them, which tumbled down onto the floor of the cupboard. Brendan scrambled into the gap. "Yes, I can get through now," he said, edging himself out. He was down on the floor of the cupboard. He reached back and helped Dessy through, then Billy.

"We've got to move fast," he said, setting off towards the stairs.

"Hey, we left our spikes behind," said Dessy.

"Too late to go back now," said Brendan, and they all rushed up the stairs.

When Molly opened the basement door at the top of the stairs, she was just in time to see Miss Carr and Dervla going out through the main door of the library. She went across to the door and cautiously looked out through the letter-box slit She could see Car-Wash's white van parked just outside the library. It was beginning to get dark now.

Suddenly she heard behind her a soft *miaow*.

"Internet," she said quietly. She bent down and stroked her. The cat began to purr.

Molly looked again through the slit in the door. The two women opened the back doors of the van. There was a jumble of boxes, suitcases and rugs inside.

She heard Miss Carr say: "We'll stow the diary in this box under the groceries. No one will find it there, even if they come looking."

She was just hiding the diary away when Dervla said: "Evanna, what about that money you said you had in the library? Did you remember to bring it?"

"We've got to hurry," said Miss Carr, "we'll leave it there."

"I don't think so," said Dervla. "We might as well have every cent we can get."

She moved back towards the library. "All right, all right," said Miss Carr impatiently, following her.

Molly looked around in panic. Dervla was at the

door. If Molly ran, she'd be spotted. She crouched down behind the door, so that it hid her when Dervla pushed it open, and Miss Carr followed. Internet dashed out into the main part of the library. The cat distracted their attention so that luckily they didn't notice Molly.

"That wretched cat pops up everywhere," said Miss Carr.

"She must be fond of you," Dervla sneered.

They both hurried into the office. Molly realised she must act at once. She crept out of the main door of the library. Car-Wash had left the back doors of the van open. Molly ran across and climbed into the back of the van. She pulled one of the rugs over herself and lay still on the floor. Suddenly Internet leaped in and burrowed under the rug beside her. Molly held her, hoping she wouldn't give a sudden *miaow* and give them away.

The two women came back, and Miss Carr shut the back doors of the van. "OK, Dervla, get in," she said. They both got into the van and it roared away up the road.

Brendan, Dessy and Billy ran across the library to the main door and pulled it open. They were just in time to see the van careering up the road.

"They got away," said Dessy. "But where's Molly?"

"She must be hiding somewhere," said Billy. They roamed around the library, looking behind bookstacks and into the office and the old computer room, calling Molly's name.

"There's no sign of her," said Brendan.

"Do you think she ran out of the main door there?" asked Dessy.

"If she did, they'd have seen her," said Brendan.

"Maybe they *did* see her," said Billy. They looked at one another in alarm.

"There's no other explanation," said Brendan. "Molly's been kidnapped!"

"We've got to tell the Guards now," said Dessy.

"And Molly's parents, first of all," said Brendan. "You and Billy go there, Dessy, and I'll run round to that Guard friend of theirs, Emma Delaney, and get her to have a search started. They'll believe us now, all right. I've got the evidence here!" He held up the polaroid photograph which clearly showed Miss Carr kneeling down and taking the diary out of the cupboard.

The van rattled and bumped as it went along the country roads. Molly was jolted about under the rug, but she held on to Internet, who fortunately decided to go to sleep.

Molly heard Dervla say: "We've got to go back to my father's pub – I've got stuff there I need to take with me to the States."

"OK," said Miss Carr, "but it's too risky to stay there tonight, just in case those kids have gone to the

Guards. Seamus's pub would be the first place they'd come looking."

"Will we go straight to the airport?" asked Dervla.

"No, we've got the tickets, we'll go to Los Angeles on the plane at half past twelve tomorrow."

"So where will we stay tonight?"

"I've thought of just the place. You know Mrs O'Rourke runs those holiday horse-drawn caravans? There's a broken-down one at the edge of a field just out of town. We'll hide out in there."

"What about the van?"

"I'm sure your father has some old tarpaulin cover we could throw over it."

"Come to think of it, he does have one of those covers they strap on over the barrels on the drink lorries."

"That'll do fine."

Molly thought she might try to slip out of the van when they stopped at Seamus Gallagher's pub, and run off to give the alarm. But when Car-Wash and Dervla got out, she heard Miss Carr say: "I'd better lock up while we go in and get your stuff. The people who drink in your father's pub are a thieving bunch, I shouldn't wonder."

"Look who's talking about thieving!" Dervla snapped.

Molly heard the locks on the van click into place. The pair went on squabbling as they moved off to the pub. Molly poked her head out from under the rug just to get a few breaths of air. Her hiding-place was stifling and mucky. The van was a tatty old vehicle – there was even a hole in the floor through which Molly could see the ground below.

She looked at the box of groceries. It was so dark she couldn't really see what was in it, but she felt around and discovered a bar of chocolate. She took it out and began to munch. Internet slept on.

It was too risky to try and break out of the van. They would probably hear the noise, and catch her. Dervla was a dangerous woman. She would stop at nothing to make sure they got away with the stolen diary. Molly would just have to stay in the van and hope to escape later on.

At first Molly's parents could hardly believe that Molly had disappeared. Brendan and Dessy told them how they had searched everywhere. The van was the only place she could be. Locky was there and he tried to calm the Donovans by saying: "If she *is* with that pair, she won't do anything stupid. Molly's a brave girl, she won't panic. And it's very unlikely they'll do her any harm. I wouldn't be surprised if she gives them the slip and turns up here before long." But he didn't sound as confident as he would like to be.

After Brendan had seen Emma Delaney, she and other Guards were quickly round at the Donovans' house. Brendan and Dessy gave them all the information they had, about the hidden diary and the plans to sell it for a fortune in California.

The Guards rang Joan Bright to get further information about the diary, then made their plans. Emma was to wait here at Molly's house in case the kidnappers made contact. The Guards would go round to Seamus Gallagher, and see what he knew about his daughter's whereabouts. If he couldn't or wouldn't tell them, they'd mount a search. If they couldn't find them tonight, at least they knew they planned to catch the Los Angeles flight the next day. They could pick them up at the airport.

Brendan was able to telephone his father secretly and let him know what was happening. He said the press weren't supposed to know anything, so it would be best to keep it secret, so that he could get a real scoop for the paper. His father sounded very excited. Brendan realised that getting such a story could make a big difference to whether he would keep his job. He said he would ring his father again as soon as there was anything new to report.

"Thanks a lot, Brendan," his father said. "You're a great fella. Meanwhile, I won't say a word, and mind you keep looking out for Molly."

"I will, dad," said Brendan, "I'm sure she'll be OK." Like Locky, he wished he really *was* as sure as he said.

Molly and Internet were jolted around even more than before, as Miss Carr switched off the van's lights and drove it across the field to the derelict caravan in the corner. She stopped it just beside the caravan, and the two women got out. To Molly's horror, she heard the back doors of the van open. She held her breath and kept totally still, curled up under the rug. Amazingly, Internet had slept through the entire journey, and didn't even wake up now.

Molly heard Miss Carr groping in the box of groceries and pulling out the hidden diary. Then she slammed the van doors shut and locked them. There was no way of getting into the front of the van and out that way – it was blocked off by a metal barrier. She thought she might be able to prise the back doors open somehow, but then she got a shock.

She heard a flapping sound on the roof of the van, and heard Miss Carr say: "There, that's got the tarpaulin over it. We'll tie the ends round the wheels, then no one will see it."

Molly was trapped: locked in, and wrapped up, like a parcel! It was going to be a long and uncomfortable night.

Emma Delaney sat up with Molly's parents, who took it in turns to get some sleep. Brendan and Dessy tried to sleep but they could only doze in their beds, waiting all the time for the telephone to ring with news of Molly. Billy slept on the sofa as best he could.

The Guards told them that Seamus Gallagher claimed he hadn't seen anything of his daughter for a long time. As far as he knew, he said, she was in the USA. As for Miss Carr the librarian, he didn't even know her. He told the Guards they were welcome to search the whole place. Unfortunately for him, they did it so thoroughly that they found a couple of stolen television sets and a stereo unit which he had hidden in the cellar. They took them away and said they would charge him in due course: there were more important things on their mind at the moment.

Wisely, Car-Wash and Dervla had not told him where they planned to hide out, or Seamus might well have offered to trade the information if they would ignore the stolen goods.

It was eight o'clock in the morning when Molly was woken by the sound of the tarpaulin being pulled off the van. Then she heard the van being unlocked. The doors were opened and Miss Carr pushed a brief-case under the rug. It just touched Molly's foot, but Miss Carr didn't notice.

"That's the diary well hidden," she said. Then she called to Dervla in the caravan: "OK, let's go!"

"Not till I've made a cup of coffee," Molly heard Dervla say. "There's plenty of time."

"The sooner we're away from here, the better," said Miss Carr sharply. "You can get some coffee at the airport. *Come on!*" She heard Miss Carr move away and go up the steps that led into the caravan. The van doors were still open. Molly decided she would have to make a run for it. She jumped down from the van, and snatched the briefcase from under the rug. Just then Internet leaped out of the van and gave a big yawn, then a loud *miaow*.

Miss Carr heard it and looked out of the caravan.. "What on earth are *you* doing here?" she snapped. Internet ran off across the field and Molly set off after her. But it was too late. Miss Carr had spotted her, and with surprising agility she jumped down off the steps and ran after Molly. She caught up with her and grabbed the briefcase.

"Where did you spring from, you horible little pest?" she shouted. "Give that to me!"

There was a tug-of-war with the briefcase, but Miss Carr was too strong. Molly felt it slipping out of her hands. Miss Carr gave a final wrench at it, stumbled backwards and fell flat on her back in the mud. Before she could get up again, Molly sprinted off across the field.

"Come back here!" Miss Carr yelled, but by the time she had scrambled up, Molly was nearly at the gate. Soon she was in the road, and running towards the town and her parents' house. She heard Miss Carr shouting to Dervla: "Hurry! Hurry! We've got to get out of here!"

Molly had never seen such rejoicing as she did when she staggered in at the door, muddy and bedraggled. Everyone hugged her, firing questions at the same time.

Emma got on her mobile phone to alert the Guards that Molly was safe. They had been planning to station a couple of squad cars near the airport road, as well as having Guards at the airport itself, so that they could stop the white van as soon as it was spotted.

"They're all delighted you're safe," said Emma. "and now we know you're OK, the chief has decided to change the plan, and let the pair of them go into the airport with the briefcase. They'll arrest them at the check-in desk – that way they'll be caught red-handed with the diary and it will prove they planned to steal it and take it out of the country."

Brendan said he would go and phone his parents to let them know Molly was safe. He was also able to tell his father about the plan to make the arrest at the airport. "I'll be there," his father said. "What a story! Thanks a lot, Brendan."

Locky said: "Into my car, Ballygandon Gang! You're the ones who got them found out, you deserve to be there at the Grand Finale!"

Molly's mother said: "Molly, you've got to rest, you've had a terrible ordeal . . ."

"I feel just fine, Mam," said Molly, and I wouldn't miss this for the world!"

Locky's car rattled along with the four of them crammed into it. Molly said that Internet had done such great detective work, she had to come too, so she was cradling the cat on her lap, in the front seat. They kept behind the unmarked Garda car which was following the white van along the road to the airport.

The white van went into the short-term multi-storey car park, and the Garda car followed. So did Locky. They could see the Guards on their mobile phone, alerting their colleagues inside the airport. Locky parked a couple of rows away from the van, and they waited until Car-Wash and Dervla got out. They got a suitcase each out of the back of the van. Miss Carr was also carrying the briefcase with the diary in it.

When the two women had gone down in the lift to go to the Departures area, Locky and the Ballygandon Gang followed, keeping their distance. The Garda car had driven out of the car park.

Inside the airport, there was a big crowd of people wheeling trolleys crammed with luggage, many of them looking puzzled as they gazed at the information boards telling you where to check in for each destination. The Ballygandon Gang saw the Aer Lingus flight to Los Angeles listed, and moved towards the area.

Molly wasn't sure she was allowed to bring a cat in without a cage of some kind, so she put Internet into her tote-bag and hoped she would keep quiet. The cat gazed up at her with her yellow eyes, then curled up in the bottom of the bag.

Locky and the Ballygandon Gang watched from behind a batch of trolleys a little distance away, as Miss Carr and Dervla wheeled their luggage trolley up to the check-in desk. Brendan looked across at the queues for the other desks, and noticed his father standing in one of them, writing in a notebook. His father saw him, and smiled. Then he gave the thumbs-up sign. Brendan did the same.

They saw the airline clerk look at Miss Carr and Dervla Gallagher, then glance to one side at a man in a dark suit standing near the next desk. They saw the man nod.

The clerk checked in their suitcases and the cases went away on the moving belt towards the aircraft. Miss Carr held on to her briefcase.

The clerk tapped away at her keyboard, checking the seats on her screen, then put the tickets and boarding passes on the counter in front of her. Miss Carr was about to pick them up, when the man in the dark suit came forward.

"Excuse me, madam," he said, holding out an identification card, "I am Detective Inspector O'Keefe. I'd like to have a look at your briefcase please."

"What's wrong?" said Miss Carr. "We've done nothing."

Locky and the Ballygandon Gang watched Miss Carr clutching her briefcase as she argued, trying to bluff her way out of the situation.

"The briefcase, please, madam," said the detective, holding out his hand and grasping it firmly. Miss Carr tried to hold on, but he took it from her. He opened it and took out Princess Ethna's diary.

"Is this your property?" he asked.

"Of course it is!" Miss Carr blustered. "It's just some old papers of mine with some scrawled notes on them."

"Really?" said the detective. He beckoned to another man in a suit standing near one of the other check-in desks. The man came over. With him was a small, plump woman with glasses. It was Joan Bright the librarian.

The first detective showed her the diary and she examined it, smiling. Then she said: "Yes, this is the original document."

Miss Carr shouted: "This woman is talking rubbish! That's mine, I tell you. It's my notes for a lecture I'm giving in America."

Joan Bright said calmly: "Do you always make your notes in Old Irish?"

The detective told Miss Carr and Dervla: "We'd like you to come with us, please."

A uniformed Guard came to join them. Dervla looked round her in panic. "Run for it!" she cried. But she had only taken two steps when the guard seized her by the arms and held her back. Miss Carr was luckier. She sprinted off across the big hall, knocking over trolleys and dodging in and out among the throng of passengers.

She was heading for the escalator that led down to the Arrivals Hall and the exit.

The first detective was soon on his mobile phone to alert other Guards around the airport. The second detective chased after Miss Carr, and he was joined by several airport security officials – *and* by the entire Ballygandon Gang, with Locky as well as Brendan's father.

Passengers watched in surprise as the great chase went down the escalator, squeezing past the people on it and stumbling over cases. In the Arrivals Hall, Miss Carr headed for the exit doors, then saw that there were Guards and security people at all of them. They began to rush towards her. She turned and ran through the door that led to the luggage area where passengers arrive. The whole procession followed. Inside, Miss Carr seized a trolley and turned it round. She pushed it at her pursuers, to the astonishment of the crowd of passengers waiting to collect their luggage from the moving carousels.

Molly and the others fanned out to surround Miss Carr, who stood beside one of the carousels looking round her in panic. Suddenly she screamed, as Internet leaped out of Molly's tote-bag and onto Miss Carr's shoulder, spitting and scratching.

"Get that cat away from me!" she shouted, trying to push Internet off her. She moved backwards, and tripped. She lost her balance and fell back onto the moving carousel among the bags and cases, with Internet still clinging to her. Molly jumped on to the carousel and so did Brendan. Molly knelt down and held on to Miss Carr's, feet, while Brendan pinned down her shoulders. Internet sat on her stomach, still hissing.

The carousel moved on, until one of the Guards

went to the emergency switch and stopped it. The watching passengers applauded, as Molly lifted the cat away, and Miss Carr scrambled off the carousel, to be led away by the waiting officers.

There was a big celebration back at Brendan's family's house in Dublin, where they were all going to stay the night. They bought some special cat-food as a treat for Internet.

Brendan's father had come back to say that the editor of the paper was delighted with his exclusive story and would put it on the front page.

They phoned Molly's family and Mrs Bantam, then Locky made a call to Horseshoe House. When he came back into the room, he said: "Mrs Boyd told me to tell you there was suddenly a new message on the computer screen.

"I wrote it down," said Locky. "Here it is."

Brendan read out the letters from the piece of paper:

S G Z M J   X N T !

Quickly Brendan used the code to translate. Then he said: "However weird it may seem, I think there's only one person this can be from."

"What does it say?" asked Molly.

Brendan smiled and said: "It says: THANK YOU!"

THE END

Published by Poolbeg